Telltale:
11 stories

Edited and with an introduction by
Gwee Li Sui

DALKEY ARCHIVE PRESS
CHAMPAIGN / LONDON / DUBLIN

Originally published as *Telltale: Eleven Stories* by Ethos Books, Singapore, in 2010

Copyright © 2010, 2012 by Ethos Books

First Dalkey Archive edition, 2013
All rights reserved

Library of Congress Cataloging-in-Publication Data

Telltale : 11 Stories / edited by Gwee Li Sui. -- First Dalkey Archive edition.
      pages cm
   ISBN 978-1-56478-905-1 (acid-free paper)
1. Short stories, Singaporean (English) I. Gwee, Li Sui, 1970- editor of compilation.
   II. Title: 11 stories.
   PR9570.S52T45 2013
   823'.010895957--dc23
                              2013030647

Partially funded by a grant from the Illinois Arts Council, a state agency

With the Support of

www.dalkeyarchive.com

Cover: design and composition by Mikhail Iliatov

Printed on permanent/durable acid-free paper

Contents

Introduction: Stories and Their Secrets
Gwee Li Sui
7

Birthday
Alfian bin Sa'at
16

In the Quiet
Tan Mei Ching
31

Haze Day
Jeffrey Lim
43

Thirteen Ways of Looking at a Hanging
Alfian bin Sa'at
58

The Drowning
Dave Chua
74

Understudies
Jeffrey Lim
92

Video
Alfian bin Sa'at
118

The Judge
Claire Tham
132

Manila Calling
David Leo
146

Much Ado About Crows
David Leo
154

Trick or Treat
David Leo
164

Notes
177

Acknowledgments
183

Contributors
185

Introduction:
Stories and Their Secrets

Gwee Li Sui

In our most essential form, as not citizens, professionals, students, parents, or children but mere humans, our fascination with stories does not come as a choice. When we are not reading a book or the news or following some drama on stage, on screen, or in a narration, we are involved in our own generation of stories that are either purely imaginative or about our otherwise dull and chaotic lives. These stories to which we contribute on a daily basis do not always appear to us as stories in view of their entanglement with our deep-seated understanding of self. Nationhood, globalisation, social and cultural identity, religious beliefs, modes of knowledge, family life, and personal ambition are all different kinds of storytelling we participate in. Thus, when we encounter a tale that actually declares itself as a tale, we do well to be a little more careful and reflect on what is here that must exceed our immediate enjoyment.

Consider the following short story that has been regarded by many as among the most perfect in the English language despite its economy of words and formal simplicity. The tale is written like the confession of a man who we recognise as mentally disturbed not just because of the unusual excitement and forwardness in the manner he speaks. This narrator may be intelligent, articulate, and very engaging, but he seems often uncomfortable with his own sanity, choosing repeatedly to test and confirm his fitness of mind with us. The oddity is telling and keeps us wary enough to avoid quick judgements and wait for more information to arrive via the narration. What we soon learn horrifies us: the speaker has, in fact, planned and just committed a murder, chopping up the body and hiding its parts under the floorboards of a house.

On every account, this shocking murder has been perfect; there is no clue left by the killer to connect him to any wrongdoing. Its execution has also been planned with such great care that even the victim sensed and communicated no danger for days until it was too late. Police officers, who then come a-knocking to investigate a neighbour's claim of having heard a cry, are quickly persuaded that the man has only awoken from a nightmare. Emboldened by these successes, the murderer continues to talk in part to brag and in part to stay assured that everything still lies within his control. The more he shares though, the more he thinks that he is hearing some unnatural heartbeat pound louder and louder from under the floorboards. By the time the story ends, convinced of the officers' actual suspicion, the man confesses to his crime and reveals exactly where he has concealed the body.

You may know this somewhat strange but riveting story as "The Tell-Tale Heart", written by the Victorian master of mystery and the macabre, Edgar Allan Poe, and first published in 1843. During the time of our reading, we are bound to feel both intrigued by the criminal mind and terrorised by the eerie possibility of a corpse's heart beating with growing intensity. Yet, a second after the story is over, we start to question whether the heart has twitched at all and what it is the killer must have experienced. Is it his own conscience—a faculty he has kept suppressed in his amoral mind all this while—pounding away? Is his socialised sense of right and wrong what wills him to fail in order to indict his own arrogance and moral deviance? Or has his creative passion doomed him to want to overwhelm his audience and shock the officers, then some presumed judge, reporter, doctor, or prison warden, and lastly us?

Poe's story conveys a lot of exciting thoughts, among which is the certainty that it is not simply about the perfect murder, crime and punishment, guilt, self-destructiveness, or madness. On an obvious and yet fundamental level, this is a story about stories, a parable about the way narratives function in a generic sense. What we encounter is primarily a tale with regular features: a setting, some characters, a basic plot, a climax, and a twist. More than that, the narrator's mind operates on another level that involves the complex business of struggling to master the story he is conjuring in real time and we are reading. As his secret crime is itself the ground on which the story, his attempt to deceive, is built, we should find it no coincidence that, once the truth is revealed, the tale also comes to an end. We are given a very simple point: this story exists only because there is something more underneath, or, to put it differently, only because the truth remains unclear, the fiction is possible here.

In this sense, the pragmatist's usual complaint that stories are useless and do not even speak of real things must be known as a red herring. Any opposition between truth and fiction is misleading since, if truth alone had been enough, fiction itself would not have come into being in the life of human civilisation. What fiction provides is the means with which we look round the corners of reality at all kinds of social and personal human neglect: what could be or might have been or truths not said, not said enough, or cannot begin to be said. Stories allow us as readers and writers to affirm or reassess our faithfulness to our own emotions and to one another as fellow humans; they give us the capacity to experience the world that lies outside the traditions of our knowledge and the systems of our everyday certainties. Pablo Picasso is often thought to have described art as a lie that tells the truth; this notion can also explain the work of fiction, the necessary dreaming through which we may approach the complexities in truths.

Can we now not see two more common mistakes in our standard treatment of literature, one relating to the powers of authors and the other to our interpretive freedom as readers? While the talents of good writers should indeed be admired, shared, and celebrated, it remains a fantasy on our part to believe that these possess knowing control over every meaning or pattern we may find in their texts. A writer's genius and his or her thoughtfulness are not an exact fit: what Poe shows us is precisely the way less than conscious elements—especially what deviates from a writer's intentions—can sneak into the life of a story. For this reason, not just readers but writers themselves are always able to discover fresh significance whenever they engage or return to completed narratives. The understanding empowers us as readers with the certainty that we are fully permitted to interpret a story as we deem fit, so long as there is sufficient textual evidence for doing so.

That being said, we also ought to realise that readers are still not the clear receptacles who need only to draw on their own impressions and emotions to assess the depths in stories. The mistake here is a popular one, based on some notion that interpreting means feeling and that "doing literature" is just about communicating that feeling. What each act of reading does is quite subtle: it allows a reader to activate his or her own ability to enjoy a story via a private struggle, a process through which a part of him or her invariably gets left behind. Thus, as writers in the heat of creation are vulnerable to the way storytelling draws from their thoughts, emotions, and experiences, readers are open to a field of "misdirections" that relates to what they bring to the texts. This intrusion allows us to differentiate between mere reading and "doing literature", the latter being a more conscious activity that involves our intuitions as well as our willingness to test, ground, correct, and study them. Its deeper implication is exciting here: we are, in fact, brought to see readers and writers alike as characters in the drama of how stories come alive!

To stress this point, "doing literature" requires us to commit to engaging a story more than once to understand why we feel what we feel about it. Like revisiting a crime scene to piece together what appears at first as unclear clues, it is a form of detective and forensic work, a science of tracing shared emotions between a reader and a character and between readers. The actual pursuit is seldom as tedious as it may sound to someone used to treating stories like disposables, commodities to be enjoyed quickly and at leisure. Through its critical process drawing on all we know about language, society, and human life at a point in time, textual analysis rewards us with greater clarity and an inner expansion not just in the sense of having learnt more about places, people, and ourselves. Rather, we arrive at a stronger realisation that the world has never been, as the Greek philosopher Heraclitus put it, a river we can step into twice. This truth about the moment, intense and full, is what we discover especially when the terrain remains the same; in the discovery, we feel anew how life itself always invites.

* * *

This anthology brings together eleven stories by writers from Singapore that openly celebrate meaning-making in every direction, from considerations of themes, symbols, structures, and characterisation to historical and cultural grounding and opinions on life. The tales are modern ones—graphic, gritty, striking, and evocative—and they confront with unwavering focus a universe that is marked by short happiness and haunting memories. These writers stretch the tents of their imagination over an area governed by laws no less brutal than the volatility of life and the return to the modern consciousness of nature, red in tooth and claw. From the sudden loss of a parent, a child, or a friend to the menacing forces of the unexpected, their subject matters draw our hearts and minds to the sheer power of everyday emotions. The stories dare us to meet the face of our contemporary world made both dazzling and hideous by enigmatic characters who might as well have walked out of our mundane reality into the book.

Alfian bin Sa'at's skills are fiercely situated and concern teasing complexities out of familiar relationships and small settings. Often refusing to disturb his fictional environments, he chooses rather to penetrate his characters' psyches in an attempt to show them torn between responsibilities and desires, between culture and individuality. "Birthday" and "Video" exhibit in this way the day-to-day dynamics of two very different Malay families as they explore what intimacy and change may require of them. Both stories use a central device to frame a delicate slice of time: the first introduces a working mother's idea of a birthday gift for her best friend to illustrate her quiet bid for understanding. The second turns a video camera owned by the late head of a household into a thing of marvel, a third eye through which its other members seek to comprehend life and to remember the dead.

Alfian also contributes "Thirteen Ways of Looking at a Hanging", one of two stories proudly published for the first time in this collection. At times objective and at times personal, the tale offers a wildly inventive look at the slow and gruelling hours of a prisoner who is on death row. We are invited to imagine, with the help of our own inner resource as fellow humans, a very imperfect man and the life of his mind in confinement and without redemption. Meanwhile, Dave Chua's "The Drowning", another new short story included here, offers a cinematic experience of the horror of the Indian Ocean tsunami of 2004 through the anguish of a family. The catastrophe is, in fact, used deftly to address something more, other forms of dying that may not be as visible or enormous but are devastating nonetheless. Both Alfian's and Chua's creations ought to be read as tragedies and cautionary tales on one level and philosophical confrontations with life on another.

Tan Mei Ching's "In the Quiet" seems at first glance only to involve a lighter reality that takes us back to our childhood days, a time when happiness felt surer and innocence more concrete. She soon perversely introduces into this garden of delight the shadow of death, and we are forced to wonder how the innocent cope with life's nastiness and to address the mental choices we each make to "grow up".

Jeffrey Lim shares two markedly dissimilar stories that are united by the sheer technical cunning he demonstrates in their framing. While one story focuses on an environmental reality familiar to residents of Singapore in recent decades, the country in the other is only vaguely recognisable as a backdrop reimagined along cheeky science-fictional lines. "Haze Day" observes one fateful day in the separate lives of four individuals, the period being coincidentally marked out by the arrival of haze from the forest fires in Indonesia. The portrayal of layers in "Understudies" is a different sort and relates to the functioning of a society where simple mistakes and deviations from social norms are not tolerated. The story allows us to confront the assumptions behind our own sense of community, the kind of society and future we truly want, and the cost we ought to be prepared to bear for our expectations.

Discerning readers should be able to tell by now that this anthology involves an artistic generation born after Singapore achieved full political independence in 1965. All six writers grew up in an environment where the literary traditions of the West prevailed over local artistic sensitivities both in school and in society. They are also familiar with works by older storytellers such as Catherine Lim, Suchen Christine Lim, Philip Jeyaretnam, and Simon Tay, whose regular attention to issues of national history and identity only suggests to them evidence of some creative markers. The questions they then go on to ask are distinct: why should writing in Singapore be damned either to serve the project of nation-building directly or to compose exotica, the kind that floods Western markets about the East? Why are those who are able to define and shape this field bent on standardising it in an ultimately self-defeating act that reveals the dark underside of postcolonial "freedom"?

As the authors are clearly writing in ways that accompany such dissatisfaction, I have planned from the start for the anthology to make a clean break from earlier collections which have stressed national themes or asserted some sense of community. What we must now acknowledge is that this kind of attention can be a trap, its emphasis on "Singaporeanness" installed at the cost of creative and academic focus stagnating along the same lines for too long. Indeed, the work unwittingly turns Singaporean literature into a navel-gazing activity with narrow concerns and predetermined debates when the hearts of its best writers are far larger and often far more universal. With such a wish to broaden consciousness and possibilities, my edition has done the radical work of relegating any issue of "placeness" to the domain of explanatory notes found in its closing pages.

In the course of my work here, I have received the assistance and support of several individuals who simply cannot be left unacknowledged. My appreciation extends to those from the Curriculum Planning and Development Division of the Ministry of Education in Singapore, who have given me valuable advice. Michele Thompson, Koh Jau Chern, and May Tan from the National Arts Council have been generous with their help on a number of crucial administrative fronts. Last but not least, publisher Fong Hoe Fang, Adeleena Araib and Leo Tong Juan, have shown themselves to be remarkable professionals in their respective fields. In view of what now needs to be read to be believed, I leave in your hands this modest but powerful book, whose spine I hope you will bend for a long time yet to read and reread its stories for their secrets.

Birthday

Alfian bin Sa'at

"I'm not asking you to pawn off your jewellery," Rosminah's husband tells her.

Rosminah picks out a fifty-dollar note from her purse, the equivalent of two days' work. It had been folded neatly into one special corner of her purse. It was to be used to buy her friend Kala a birthday present. For Rosminah's birthday, Kala had given her a sandwich maker. Rosminah had opened it with care, taking her time with the scotch tape. She had later used the wrapping paper to line her drawers.

It was enamel white, the sandwich maker, and there was a yellow light that blinked when the bread was done. The sandwiches it made were triangles with crispy sides and soft insides, which Rosminah fills with Kraft cheese or Ayam Brand sardines. Her husband brings the sandwiches to work, which Rosminah packs, in aluminium foil.

"I'll pay it back by the end of the month," says her husband as Rosminah places the money by his side. She is used to his lying. Or forgetting, which to Rosminah was no different. She is also used to his anger when she places the money directly into his hand, with her eyes looking into his face such that he has to turn away. At one such instance, his face had crumpled and he flew into a rage, asking Rosminah if she really thought that he was poor, that he really needed her money that badly.

Birthday

Before the wind could blow it off the bed, her husband picks up the note and slips it into his shirt pocket.

"How are the children?" he asks next, cocky and unable to stay silent. Rosminah clasps the button on her purse with a click which she will remember days later. With patience she replies, talking to the reflection of her husband in the bedroom mirror.

"They are all right."

"Any problems in school?"

"No."

"Anything for me to sign?"

"No. Nothing."

"I don't sign if I see red marks."

"Our children don't get red marks."

"I know. I just don't sign if I see that they have been lazy."

"Our children aren't lazy."

"I know." Her husband pauses to compose himself. "I know all that, you don't have to tell me." Her husband then starts to yawn. It could have been a real yawn or he could have made it up. Whatever it was, he tells Rosminah that he is sleepy and tells her to switch off the lights. Rosminah walks to the light switch and wonders why all her fingers can do tonight is obey. In the dark, she hears her husband's voice, familiar yet distant at the same time.

"You're not sleeping?"

"I don't feel like it's time yet to sleep."

"What time is it now?"

"I think it's already twelve. But I don't feel like sleeping."

"You just lie down and close your eyes. When you open them it will be morning."

"Maybe I will go take a look at the children."

"They are all sleeping. What is there to look at?"

"Maybe I will light the mosquito coil in their room. Tonight there are many mosquitoes."

"I don't feel any mosquitoes. But if there are, you light one for this room too. And then you come and sleep."

"I know, after I light the mosquito coils."

"Tomorrow you must wake up."

"You have to wake up also. You have to wake up earlier than me. I will sleep later."

Rosminah's husband keeps quiet for a long time and drifts off to sleep. He sleeps with a fifty-dollar note in his shirt pocket. He might or might not crumple it, but in the morning it will still be there. For a moment, Rosminah wants to march back to her husband, demand her money back, insist that she had saved it up for someone else. But the thought of having nothing to say when he turns and grumbles, except a half-spoken apology, angers her. She turns to walk into the children's room.

The room is half-lit by orange streetlamps outside the window. A gentle wind rhythmically pushes the curtains into the room. The children are sleeping on a mattress side by side; Mohd Rosli with his head buried under his pillow, and Siti Nuraini's half-open mouth facing the sole-smeared wall. There is a study desk beside the mattress with a blackened fluorescent tube that flickers when it is switched on and marker scrawlings of both the children's names on the mock pine finish. Attached to the desktop are shelves that hold dog-eared school textbooks and Happy Meal toys (a Dalmatian popping from a box, a bear grinning on a scooter), as well as some Games Day trophies for beanbag races and individual sprinting.

On the sides of the desks are stickers: kittens and football players, and even a Neighbourhood Watch one that was meant for the front door. Some of the stickers are half-peeled, as if at one time there was an attempt to scrape them all off. They have left fibrous stains on the wood and fingernail scars where the pine grains show through.

The children seem to be breathing in unison, just like brothers and sisters should. When Siti Nuraini was still two years old, Rosminah had taught her four-year-old brother how not to be envious and to pat his sister's backside as she cradled a bolster so she would fall asleep. Mohd Rosli even cried when Siti Nuraini had chickenpox, when he watched purple iodine lotion speckling her body. But ever since they started going to school, they would often shout at each other. Two nights ago, Mohd Rosli even went as far as to kick his sister's shin. Rosminah bends to check if the bruise is still there and touches Siti Nuraini's calf. Siti Nuraini stirs and frowns, then her face relaxes again.

In the morning, she had brought Rosminah's brooch to school and had lost it. She had come home crying, and Rosminah had beaten her on her back and shoulders. Mohd Rosli had asked her what ECA he should join. He was thinking of the Cadet Scouts since his best friend Azmi was joining it. When Rosminah found out that a complete uniform set would cost forty dollars, she told him flatly: "No." Watching them sleeping as the shadow of window grilles falls across their frail bodies, Rosminah wonders how anyone can actually beat or refuse such children. She had done both.

Rosminah thinks about the four people in her life: her husband, the two children, and Kala. Kala she had met on the first day at the factory where they made semiconductor parts. At that time, Rosminah was five months pregnant with Siti Nuraini. It was the night shift, and Rosminah was wondering whether Mohd Rosli had gone to sleep. She felt strange wearing her black apron over her large belly. The women around her all had rough faces and some of them laughed too loudly, showing off gold fillings. Kala herself was a large woman, with bulging eyes and messy hair. When she smiled, her dark gums showed. When Rosminah first sat down, a Malay woman opposite started talking to her.

"You're new here, right? I never see your face before."

Rosminah nodded. She was trying to remember what her

supervisor had told her about the resistors. Her hands were cold.

"You know what we are making?" asked the woman. She had a scarf on and kohl-rimmed eyes.

"Not sure," Rosminah replied.

"All this, is part of a rocket. We are all here making rocket parts. All this they will later send to USA."

"Really?"

"Yah. You know, rocket, to fly to the moon? People don't know some parts they make here in Bedok." The woman was smiling. "So must do your work properly, don't daydream a lot, later something explode in outer space."

"Ju!" A voice rang out from behind Rosminah. "Ju, what are you telling her? Hey, whoever that is, don't listen to Ju. She only like to disturb people. She's making fun of you only. Don't listen to her."

"What lah, Shida! I was just enjoying myself, have fun with this new girl, you must disturb! As if the work here isn't boring enough. People want to have some fun also you must interfere." The woman with the scarf then got back to her work after shouting at her friend and then smiling one more time at Rosminah.

After an hour Rosminah felt tired. The rest were drinking coffee to stay awake, but Rosminah didn't take coffee. Again she wondered whether Mohd Rosli had gone to sleep. Rosminah felt like crying. She then forced a smile, as if it would blunt her sadness, but it managed only to sharpen it. She held on to a smile for a few seconds and then let go, and her face was washed again in self-pity. She did this exercise several times, convinced that it would do her some good.

"Oi," a voice came from her left.

Rosminah froze. The Indian woman was talking to her.

"You eating what?" The Indian woman asked.

Rosminah could not help but smile. "Nothing."

"*Sotong* ah? If got some *sotong* share lah. I also like *sotong*."

"No, not *sotong*."

"Then what?"

"Nothing."

"My name is Kala. What's your name?"

"Rosminah."

"You like working here so far?"

"Okay lah. Can."

"I work here three months already. Still cannot get used. Very sleepy lah."

"Yah."

"You talk to me, then won't fall asleep. I can talk Malay. Last time my neighbour Malay. So I learn."

"It's okay. Last time I go to English school."

Kala pointed at Rosminah's round belly.

"How many months, that one?"

"Five."

"Got name already? Boy or girl? Got buy the bed already or not? I know where can get cheap. My cousin got furniture shop."

Rosminah did not know which of Kala's questions to answer, and in which order. She simply smiled, not knowing what else she could do. Suddenly, she felt a kick in her belly. Rosminah turned to look at Kala.

"She know we are talking about her," said Rosminah.

"It's a girl?"

"Yah. I got one boy already. So this one, one sister for him. I always want girl, because boys are lazy."

Kala laughed loudly, and her gums showed.

"Girls are good," said Kala, showing Rosminah her thumb.

"Can stay with you in the kitchen, can learn to cook, then you can tie their hair before they go to school."

"Yah. You got girls?"

"I'm not married. Who want to marry me? Eyes so big, laugh like man. Who want to have children with me? Later come out eyes big-big. Scare everybody."

When she heard Kala say those words, Rosminah would have been silent if not for the fact that Kala was laughing loudly, like a man. Rosminah learnt that Kala was quick to laughter because she had grown up in an orphanage. By the week after, Rosminah and Kala became good friends. In the canteen they sat next to each other, and Rosminah thought of the times she had spent in primary school. She had stopped schooling in primary four because her father, a sailor, had gone missing. She had then gone on to help her mother sell food at the railway station; they made *lontong* and *mee rebus*, and the people there called Rosminah *adik*.

While sitting in the factory canteen waiting for her food, Rosminah would wonder what had happened to all her primary school friends, whether any of them would remember her, the girl who had left too soon. But when Kala walked towards her table balancing a tray with sugarcane drinks and some hawker food, biting her tongue (Kala's habit, as Rosminah had found out within minutes of their first meeting), Rosminah knew that it was possible to make up for lost time.

For the past three nights, Rosminah had not slept. After her husband started snoring, she would creep out of the room and walk into the kitchen. Kala's birthday was just the week after, and Rosminah would open up the newspapers to see which of the department stores had sales. She saw a fruit juice maker from the Oriental Emporium that caught her eye. There was also a steam iron that came at a bargain, but it was only sold at Sogo, which was somewhere far away in town.

She could not put down the reasons for her excitement. In her wallet was fifty dollars, something she had painstakingly saved up for the past six months. She had skipped late night supper breaks at work, always telling Kala that she was full, sometimes bringing food to work: a packet of chick peas or some melon seeds. Maybe her eagerness had something to do with the thrill of having been able to save up so much money and then the scandalous thought of spending it not on herself but on someone else. What would her husband think?

Or maybe it was because she had never bought anyone a gift before. She had bought toys for her children, but always in their presence, always because they had pointed at something dangling from a raffia string tied in front of a provision shop, some action figurine or doll (Siti Nuraini had one whose eyelashes could flick open and close depending on whether it was standing or horizontal). And Rosminah had bought the toys to silence them, sometimes suspecting that they had asked for the toys purely out of boredom, and feeling annoyed that all she had bought were some kitchen towels or wooden pegs that cost only about a tenth of the toy's price.

But this gift for Kala was something different. It was to be done in secret; Rosminah would have to make sure that it would be a surprise. Was that what Rosminah wanted? Surprise? Kala's eyes growing wider than they already were, the painted finger nails caressing the gift, shaking it perhaps, bringing it close to the ear; Rosminah had recreated the scene a hundred times in her head. It was morning, the end of their shift, and at the lockers Rosminah would tell Kala to wait awhile, there seemed to be something stuck in her own locker. She would ask Kala to take a look, and Kala would see the thing wrapped in a flower-patterned wrapping paper with a bow on it. Kala would take it out and then the stage would be set. Kala's characteristic "Aiyoo" rang sharp in Rosminah's ears, the blabber of "For me ah? You sure or not? Hah? Why you never tell me ... why ... you never ... aiyoo ...

how much?" It was a form of revenge, of course. On many other occasions, Kala had been the one to surprise Rosminah.

Rosminah walks to the kitchen and sits down. The house is in complete darkness, but she can find her way around because she has lived in their three-room flat for eleven years, and also because there is not much furniture around. While walking from the children's bedroom to the kitchen, a few things had caught Rosminah's eye: the glowing digits on the VCR, the orange feline eye of the Airpot set to "warm", the red squares that pulse on the plugs that keep the refrigerator and water heater alive. Rosminah knows that some of her appliances were wedding presents, but to her, that seemed such a long time ago; she and her husband unearthing crystalware, Queen Anne's silver, and counting out money, so much money that they uncreased and sorted into bundles. It seemed then that everything they would ever need was in that room. They had money, they had a bed with coiled springs, they were the first ones from their families who had a table lamp, they had a new white satin bedsheet they might just use that night and store away forever, they had each other. Of course, the bedsheet stayed for one week, another, and after a while the pristine whiteness was gone, and it acquired a smell.

In the quiet of the kitchen, the refrigerator hums soothingly. Rosminah fixes herself some orange squash and settles into one of the kitchen stools. Those lights still going on during the night, still blinking. Wedding gifts, the VCR and Airpot, and the rice cooker and electric kettle, which are not turned on at the moment. Rosminah wonders; if she had a hundred electrical appliances and set them running all at the same time, would their small function lights flood her kitchen like an entire constellation? Maybe they could form a shape, like neon letters in the dark, a sign, lucid answers. Her question: Did she love the man she married? Or should the question be: Did she marry the man she loved? All she remembered of the wedding was her husband sitting cross-legged, in front of the *kadi*, having to say "I, Awang Bin Razali, receive Rosminah Binte Abdullah, with a dowry of fifty dollars, cash down." He had stuttered a few times before he finally got it right, even at one time saying Awang Bin Abdullah and Rosminah Binte Razali, to much laughter. When he finally got it right, the witnesses had chuckled heartily and shouted "*Sah!*" and then patted him on his back. Rosminah takes another sip from her glass. She had cost her husband fifty dollars.

"You ever come here before?" was what Kala had asked her.

Rosminah shook her head. In the distance, she could see shophouses scarred with strips of neon. There was an unearthly pink glow that came from them. When she looked over the railings she saw the river, with its slimy muscles dragging a bumboat towards them. There was a red light in the bumboat, and Rosminah could spot an old Chinese man smoking. He didn't look up at her. Near the banks the white lamps stitched wrinkles of light on the water.

"Last time he take me here," Kala said.

"Your boyfriend?" Rosminah asked.

"Don't call him that. I don't know where he is now. Nobody pick up the phone anymore. Except three nights ago. That time was the last time."

"Why you bring me here?"

"He bring me here last time," Kala said. "We sit here."

Rosminah tried to lean forward to peer into the water, but a sudden burst of light momentarily blinded her. She realised that the light came from the fluorescent tubes that lit up the bridge at night, such that from afar it seemed to possess a cold ivory glow.

"He put his hand on my leg," Kala said, and Rosminah

wondered if it was the river or herself that was pulling out words from Kala's lips. "I push his hand away, I laugh. He said I laugh like a little girl."

"What did he say?" Rosminah asked. "What did he tell you over the phone?"

Kala was about to sigh, but turned it into a smile. "He said he already has a wife. In India."

"Oh."

"He didn't want to tell me her name. He said, not important. I asked if I was important. He said, yes, of course. If not why I buy you things?"

Kala showed her ring to Rosminah. It was on her ring finger, a simple band, with a dull gleam.

"I ask him if he want the ring back. He said no, you keep it. He said, I'm not that sort of person. I want you to keep the ring."

"Kala."

"I'm a dirty woman, Rosminah. I feel like a dirty woman. In all my life, I never let someone get so close to me. This kind of things only girls do. I'm a woman."

"Kala. Men are like that."

"Last time at the Home, the Ma'am always said, this Kala here, eyes so big, very hard to close. That's why so hard to cry. You can do anything to Kala, but very hard for this girl to cry. But when someone do this kind of thing to you, how to hold everything inside?"

Rosminah let Kala lean on her shoulder. She had watched people on TV doing it, offering their shoulders to one another. She was not sure how she felt with Kala's body so close to her own, such that as Kala spoke in that low voice she could feel her own body resonate.

"Men are like that."

"Ros, when I saw you that day, first time, with your stomach so big, I think, I also want something like that. One day. Have my own children. I don't have parents, but who say cannot have children? I also think, this woman can be the godmother. Can teach me how to fold the napkin. Teach me how to burp the baby."

Kala started laughing.

"Ros, last time I dream so much! I want the baby to hold my finger in his hand. I want to bathe it like see on TV, hold the head very carefully. But now, I got already, I don't want anymore, Ros. I don't want. I feel empty. How can something grow inside me?"

Kala sighed. She then carefully eased the ring off her finger and held it up between her forefinger and thumb.

"It's my name," Kala said. "My name means what in Malay? Lose. I always lose. I don't know who give me this name."

Rosminah couldn't find anything to say. She looked around her and saw three bare-bodied men lowering fishing lines into the water. They were sweating, and she could see their bodies gleam. The bridge that they were standing on was called Cavenagh Bridge. There were huge beams that stretched behind them, studded with gigantic rivets. Rosminah was reminded how on the first day at the factory a woman had told her that they were assembling a rocket. She looked up and saw a full moon. It struck her that the moon should not belong only to men in rockets.

"Kala," Rosminah asked, "Kala, you have to know what you want. What do you want?"

Kala removed her weight from her friend's shoulder. She smiled at Rosminah, and then removed the pressure of her fingers from her ring. As it dropped in front of a fluorescent tube, it flashed for a moment, before being swallowed up by the darkness and the river whose depth neither of them knew or understood.

"I want nothing."

Rosminah asked her, "You don't want anything?"

Kala said, "I want nothing."

In an hour's time, it will be dawn. The children will have to be woken up, and Siti Nuraini will ask Rosminah if she should wash her hair, and Rosminah will remind her that she had washed it the night before. Mohd Rosli will have to be woken up at the breakfast table where he will fall asleep. His mouth will be hanging open, with a piece of bread dangling from its edge, squeezed into the shape of his palate. If he isn't woken up in time, it will fall out of his mouth, sending his little sister into fits of giggling.

Rosminah opens the cupboard in the children's room and takes out a box of mosquito coils. She drags out the plastic and sees that three of the four coils are broken. Rosminah then starts cracking them up into even smaller pieces before realising that the rustle of plastic could wake her children. She stops herself firmly and thinks: *I am not well.* She looks at the broken fragments of mosquito coils in the plastic and tells herself: *There is no happiness in this world. Even if there is, none of it is mine.*

Rosminah then walks into her bedroom. Her husband is snoring. She realises that she has not slept for an entire night. Slowly, she settles into position by her husband's side. His hair is thinning, and his forearm is placed near the top of his head. Under the hairs on his armpit is a large mole. Rosminah closes her eyes. She wants to catch some sleep, even if it is for half an hour, catch whatever night there is left before birds start making noises outside. Sometimes, when Rosminah happened to be awake just at dawn, she would hear the faint twitter of invisible birds and an occasional braggart crow. Rosminah wonders if birds can feel cold, whether they climbed the morning shaking off the dew from their wings.

Sleep does not come over her. Instead, Rosminah feels a numbness that creeps up her legs, like sap, up her thighs and stomach. She winces and wonders whether it was true what her mother told her last time, that if you feel your body being frozen, paralysed, it means that an evil spirit is sitting on you. She hears frantic echoes panting, in her ears, and struggles to steer her mind away to other things.

Her friend gave her something for her birthday. She will give something back for Kala's birthday. It is only fair.

Rosminah then reaches her hands out as if in fear that the numbness would finally reach them. She gathers them from the quicksand of her body and brings them, trembling, to her face. She whispers, "Help me God," before reaching out with her left hand towards her husband's side. In the darkness she feels for his pocket, gently. She slips in her fingers and feels the crisp fifty-dollar note tucked inside. Just as she is about to pull it out, her husband clasps her hand with his own and then sighs. He says something, and then Rosminah realises that the numbness has gone, has leaked away as if through a hole that has been punctured in her side. She hears a sharp ring and knows it is the sound of the alarm clock in the children's room.

In the kitchen, all Rosminah can concentrate on are her hands. Open the bread bin. Take out the butter and *kaya* from the refrigerator. Scoop the Milo into the washed-out Nutella mugs. As she is tying Siti Nuraini's hair, she hears Mohd Rosli asking her:

"*Mak*, why are you smiling?"

After sending her children off at the door, Rosminah walks into the kitchen again. She looks out of the window and sees a sweeper pushing a trolley with rubbish bins on it. Rosminah opens the window grilles. She then leans out and feels a strange wind blowing. She walks back to the cabinet and unplugs the sandwich maker, the same one she had used to prepare her children's breakfast. Her fifty dollars is still in her husband's pocket. When he held her hand, he had asked, "Rosminah, *sayang*, you never sleep one whole night?"

Rosminah stretches her arms out of the window. The sandwich maker is heavy in her hands. Then she lets her fingers go. They obey her will. The sandwich maker falls, followed by its wire and plug trailing behind it, and for a moment, Rosminah thinks that she sees Kala's ponytail plummeting downwards. Rosminah closes her eyes and clenches her fists against the ledge. She feels something within her fly out; a lightness that lasts as long as is necessary until a bang and a shout force her to open her eyes.

She looks down to see Mohd Rosli comforting Siti Nuraini, and she sees the wreckage she has made, an enamelled casing splintered into innumerable pieces. Siti Nuraini is crying, partly because of the shock but mostly because she had recognised the sandwich maker. Mohd Rosli looks up at his kitchen window and sees Rosminah, looking down. Their eyes meet from that distance, and Rosminah mouths something. She sees on her son's face the expression she had wanted to see on Kala's; that disbelief, the shock of identifying her as Rosminah, quiet Rosminah, a birthday wish stuck between her sobs.

In the Quiet

Tan Mei Ching

The bell rang.

"Assembly's a pain in the butt," I said. 7.20 A.M. What better time to listen to A.B., Principal A-Bore, give long speeches that wound round our necks until we choked? The whole school, from Primary Ones to Secondary Fours, had to line up in the courtyard like toothpicks in a box. We fidgeted. The ground was rough cement in patches and smooth almost everywhere, probably polished by many, many shuffling feet like ours.

When we were released into church for the morning sermon, Jenny said, "Maybe if I come late, I don't have to attend assembly."

"But if you come late, the prefects will catch you, and then you have to go detention," I said.

We sighed, sitting down on the hard benches in the chapel. At least it was cooler inside. Our school was a mission school, no nun teachers in this day and age but regular teachers who got pregnant now and then, and teachers like Mrs. C. who had children, though we didn't want to imagine how she might have gotten them. The morning (yawning) session started. As always, the Reverend talked into his Bible and gestured dramatically with his free hand. A few of us at the back watched Ellen. She sat perfectly still for the first few minutes, then her head nodded more and more heavily. "Let us sing Hymn 160," the Reverend said. Ellen woke up long enough to stand, but, right into the first line of the hymn, she started nodding and almost fell over. Audrey, out of the kindness of her youth, put out a hand to steady her. The rest of us tried to keep a straight face.

School was the place to cultivate the art of getting out of things. Getting out of class before the bell rang—"Teacher, must go toilet, very high tide." Getting out of doing homework—"That chapter was done in my old exercise book. Really. I threw it away already." Getting out of classroom duties—"Pick up the big rubbish, dust you can't see, floor is grey what."

"How to get out of Maths class?" I asked rhetorically as we filed out of church for classes.

Audrey said, "I have a way!"

"Huh?" I wanted her to elaborate, but E.T. was already in class, writing out sums on the blackboard.

"Yuck, cockroach!" someone said. Immediately, someone else shrieked. I saw something brown scuttling across the floor and stepped on it. It got mushed. "Yuck!" Ellen said. I shrugged. I wasn't afraid of spiders or lizards or rats either, dead or alive. I wasn't even afraid of teachers.

"Come here." Mrs. Chew, alias E.T., gestured to me when we sat down and took out our books. "Why didn't you complete the longitude and latitude problems in the Maths test?"

"Don't like them." I could feel everyone's eyes and ears on me.

Mrs. Chew frowned. "You have to try."

"Why? I passed the test, right?"

She frowned some more, nothing to say. I could feel the respect barometer rise in the class.

"*Wah*, you very brave," Audrey told me after class, turning around in her seat just in front of me.

"Hey, what plan you got to escape assembly?" I said. Before she could tell me, Mrs. Ho came in and started Composition.

Audrey turned back to her desk. "A trip at sea," Mrs. Ho said. Some people groaned. I started writing right away. There was a dream I had always remembered. I probably had it when I was about nine. I was walking by some speckled marble seats when a great flood came and swirled me underwater. I saw glistening fishes swimming around. Somebody floated by limply. I grabbed her and tried to make for the surface. A shark came. I swam like crazy. The woman slowed me down, but I couldn't abandon her. The shark closed down on us. I cringed for the pain of sharp teeth—I was so afraid—but there was no sharp teeth, no pain—the shark had no teeth, total gum bald. The shark forgot to wear its dentures! It swallowed us whole, then spat us out, propelling us like torpedoes. This shark didn't eat dead people! I realised that the person I was carrying was long gone. I didn't know that, but she saved my life. I reached up and found a marble seat. I pulled myself out. Safe! I looked down. Everything was gone, the water, the fishes. The sidewalk was bone-dry. The water had only been as high as the marble seats. Why didn't I just stand up?

I stopped writing here. I remembered the thought that came to me in the dream all those years ago: what was appearance and apparent was deceiving; beyond the fabric of our world were other worlds, and, every now and then, paths crossed, chaos ensued, but it was only a passing, and it will pass away. Awake, I had thought: I changed the world I was in when I wanted it badly enough. I made everything work out.

"Geez, you read too many books," Jenny said over my shoulder.

I wondered how to end my composition. I couldn't write down those thoughts I had; they scared even me. So I wrote, "That was my most memorable trip at sea."

"Have you heard of Leon Uris and his book, *Exodus*?" Audrey asked, turning around in her seat again. "It's about Israel."

"War story?" I said.

"Kind of. A bit of history too, but not like what we learn in school."

"Hope not. Hope you have better taste than that."

Jenny made a face. "What's so nice about war stories?"

"Stories of strength and courage," I said. "So close to death, and people always chose life."

Audrey nodded, but Jenny didn't look convinced. The bell rang and we broke for recess.

The flies were tremendously active on the tables in the tuckshop. I rolled up some newspaper and began hitting them.

"Pretty good," Audrey remarked in admiration.

I shrugged. My cousin Paul and I used to do this when we went to chalets. Hitting flies took a certain sort of skill, a control of the arm and swiftness of the blow, sudden, merciless, complete. The trick was to approach the fly very slowly and, when almost directly above, to be so quick that the fly didn't know what was coming, didn't have a chance to react. Sometimes, Paul and I each opened up a plastic bag and caught the flies alive. We would fill up the bags with water and watch them struggle. They couldn't get free, but they struggled all the same. Then we emptied the bags into the toilet. The flies were too wet to fly and we pulled the flush immediately. There was no escape.

"So small yet so quick," Jenny said of the flies.

"Small. Did you know that if a volume of air the size of our little finger got in your bloodstream you'll have a brain haemorrhage?" I said. "Burst vessels."

Jenny frowned at me, "Why you always talk about such gross stuff?"

"I found that out when I was six and my grandmother died," I said. When Jenny made a face, I continued. "On the hospital bed, she had two tubes stuck into each arm. One was purple, the other transparent. I thought that they pumped air into her body. But of course it wasn't."

I remembered my grandmother's fingers by the bed. That was all I could see of her. I wasn't tall enough to look over the bed yet.

"Did you go to the funeral?" Audrey asked.

"Yeah, it was like something from TV. The coffin was surrounded by flowers, priests chanted prayers, people wore dull colours, spoke in low voices, and looked solemn."

"Weren't you sad at all?" Jenny asked.

"Did you cry?" Audrey asked.

"Everyone was crying," I said. I didn't ask why it was so sad. Everyone seemed to know, so I cried hard for grandma too, to show that I understood. "But not me, not really."

"So heartless," Jenny said.

It was after school and before library duty when Audrey told me what her plan for escaping assembly was. We had the first lunch break and were on our way to A&W.

"See," Audrey told me, "Wednesdays Chinese begins at 9.00. I don't have Maths at 8.00, right, because I dropped it, so I'm going to come to school at 8.45."

"What if the prefects caught you? Late five minutes one hour detention class. Late ten minutes two hours. For you, you'll have seventeen hours detention—break record, man!"

"No, *lah*. Listen. The prefects have classes at 8.00. They'll be gone by the time I reach here. And there won't be anyone around."

"Except the drink-seller."

We laughed. I noticed for the first time how neat and small her teeth were—they were all quite the same size—amazing. "You lucky pig, no Maths class." I envied her getting around assembly *and* detention in one clean, smart move. And no Maths!

At A&W, we ate fries with ketchup and chilli sauce. Then we turned our watches back, mine ten minutes and hers seven minutes behind the actual time. In case we went back late and were questioned, we could always point to our watches and say, "See? Not late what."

We didn't talk about anything much, nothing of consequence anyway. One good thing about Audrey—she didn't mind talking about things of little consequence.

Another "particularly" hot March day was here—"Isn't it par-ti-cu-lar-ly hot today?" we'd drag it out. We were, as usual, lined up for assembly. A.B. appeared at the second-story window of the hall overlooking the courtyard. She waited a moment or two, then the bell screamed like a banshee. Here we go again, I thought. A.B. looked as if she was about to say, "We are gathered here today..." which meant that she would probably embark on one of her par-ti-cu-lar-ly long subjects.

"Girls, girls, let me remind you of the importance of good behaviour while still in school uniform. The other day, I saw three girls in school uniforms at a shopping centre. They were not from our school, but I thought that it gave a very bad impression. These girls had very long hair and they didn't tie it up. Very untidy and gave a very bad impression. Schoolgirls should have neat, short hair, no perming, no tails. Also in classes, I have noticed how many girls sit. Like tomboys. Girls must learn to sit with their knees together. Girls, girls, when you don't sit properly, and the teacher stands in front to teach—what does she see? Very ugly..."

When A.B. finally let us go into the cool chapel for the "final cleansing", most of us had already perspired through our white shirts in the hot sun. My shirt stuck to my back. It was Wednesday and, since Audrey wasn't around, Ellen half-spilled over the pew in front of her. She quickly straightened up, and started to lean sideways. When we finally got out of church it was 8.10, which was good for us—ten minutes less of Maths. No complaints here. That was one nice thing about church, when it went overtime. It was better than mental anguish and psychological boredom in Maths.

When Chinese period came, our class moved into the language lab, which was the only air-conditioned room in the whole building. Loud sighs of relief as we entered. The only problem with this room was that everyone had to take off their shoes before we went in, and with about two hundred students coming in every day—phooey!—talk about palpable smells! I breathed as shallowly as I could without stopping breathing altogether. I went ahead and saved a seat for Audrey beside me. She should be coming soon, none the worse for waking up later than usual. But Chinese started with a chorus of "Good morning, Mrs. Lu," and Audrey didn't appear. Probably overslept. I hope she didn't get caught coming in late by a teacher.

Chinese was soon over. I didn't do well for the weekly Chinese "listen and write"; I forgot several characters. Usually when Mrs. Lu had the class exchange exercise books to correct each other's work, Audrey would correct mine and I hers and she would usually come out far ahead of me. Then we would sign our names in Chinese to show that we didn't mark our own books. She would sign her name with a flourish—good cause, too, with the amount of correcting she did on my page, it looked like an abstract work of art.

At first I thought the air outside was thick because for one too many times I had breathed too shallowly in the lab, but it was a strange heaviness that had nothing to do with my lungs or the par-ti-cu-lar heat and humidity, that now and then shifted, distracting in its invisibility. We stirred restlessly, our whited shoes scraping the rough cement floor of our classroom. The wind slid by low; I heard leaves rustling about the courtyard from our second floor. Something went past us; we turned our heads in unison, only to glimpse A.B.'s swishing skirt.

"Isn't this a par-ti-cu . . ." someone began.

"Shut up," someone said.

What were we keeping quiet for? Even when we filed out for recess and were jammed in the hallway just before the stairs, people were quieter than usual. Then, somewhere in front, a ripple started, a pulse of words outside my head. There was an accident out on the main street near our school. A real life accident so nearby. Anyone hurt? Not sure. Yes, I think. Was it one of the fruit-sellers by the street? Or a pedestrian?

We went about our recess, and I didn't think much about the accident—it was nearby, but didn't invade our world. I decided to call Audrey to see if she was sick. We absent ourselves now and then, in sickness and in health, so she might have just decided to skip school. It was already past ten, so Audrey probably wouldn't come to school today, and she'd probably answer the phone and say, "Hi, I overslept." As I dialled the number, I could see people milling about in the courtyard. Recess wasn't over, and already people were gathering to line up to go back to class. Strange. What's going on, I wondered. I looked at the buttons on the telephone, then at the growing crowd, and hung up. I didn't really need to know.

When I got to the courtyard, someone pulled my sleeve and whispered. "What?" I said, irritated. Again, that strange sound effect from outside my head as if I were hearing things while dreaming. They said that Audrey was in the accident. Who said? Audrey is hurt. Hurt. Dead. Dead? Wait a minute. Don't anyhow say. Are you crazy? Don't exaggerate. Don't bluff, don't anyhow say. There must be some mistake. She's probably at home. She probably skipped school today. I called her . . .

But I didn't call her. Someone poked me in the back: "Look, see A.B.'s face? It's her. Audrey."

Everyone thought that we were going back to class, but we were instructed to go to the hall. I didn't want to go. It was an odd time to feel like an actress. My role: human walking. Left leg, right hand, right leg, left hand, inhale, exhale. My real self had retreated into some dark corner, watching all of this on a monstrous silent screen that kept shifting—I'd see myself, then teachers, students trooping up the stairs, my legs and feet going up and down—shifting so my vision blurred. What was I watching? A dream and a reality crossing paths. I was caught in the passing. Which way do I go? Where do I belong?

I didn't want to enter the hall, there was a dread waiting, but I was carried along, something that could not be stopped. Whispers floated all around me. Sound of passing? Was it over? I wanted to get back where I belonged. Then, a shush like water falling when A.B. walked up to the podium. She moved the podium two inches to the left, took off her glasses, and fiddled with them. She cleared her throat and looked at us. I wished she would find herself dumb, then she couldn't say what she was going to say. I looked at her lips and wished—I wished and wished and wished—that the words tumbling out so effortlessly meant something different. There was a fatal accident near our school. A student, Audrey, of Secondary 4C was run over by a bus. Let us bow our heads and pay our respects to her in a minute of silence and prayer. I went through the words one by one, but I couldn't find any other meaning for them.

I heard people crying, softly at first, then louder, and I watched myself shrinking into my back seat. This was a crossing that would not pass. Two worlds collided and merged, and it was a new old world, born in a silence I had never heard.

It was a new world, and I expected different rules. I wanted different rules, maybe how it should change our lives, how we shouldn't be walking around doing the same old things like studying Maths and History, eating, drinking, taking the bus home. What happened on TV shows or movies at a time like this? I couldn't remember. I didn't know how I got home, I didn't see anything from the time I left school until Mom turned watery red eyes to me and I read her lips—your friend was so young. Mom, are you different? Or is it just my eyes telling me I'm wrong? I went into the bathroom, turned on the tap, and watched the water gush out. I held on to the sink and stared at the ceiling.

Audrey was on the news. They had a picture of her when she was twelve, taken from her identity card. Most strange. A story of a familiar face. Had the world of television and my world inverted, changed positions? But wait! There was no mutual consent, no consideration, no word, nothing. You know, on TV, in books, they gave you clues, a warning, a reason. There was always a reason.

Audrey was on the newspaper the next day, with the same picture. She looked much younger, but of course she was. It wasn't her at all. It was a piece from the past. This was not the face I saw two days ago. So who died? I understood about these things, I knew that I did. I knew how I should feel, and I knew that I should cry. But I just cut out the picture. I didn't have any picture of Audrey, and I wanted one, even if it wasn't the Audrey I knew.

I heard her mother had to come identify her body that morning. She didn't have to cut out any pictures. We didn't have school the next day. Buses were hired to take all the students and teachers to the funeral. The school band piled into its own bus; Audrey had played the trombone for three years. Was it the trombone? Or the drums? I'd never thought I had to remember.

At the funeral service, we went into a small hall with no windows. I was the first to approach the coffin. It was opened, but I stared straight at the wall ahead. I couldn't look into it. Ellen beside me looked into the coffin and cried into my sleeve. The band started playing and ended in a sputter because the band-girls started crying. I saw Audrey's little sisters standing near the wall beside the coffin. Did they know what happened? Did they understand? They weren't tall enough to look into the coffin, so they looked at us, to see what we saw. We filed out onto the grassy area nearby to make way for the hearse. Everyone was crying, even Mrs. C. I stood a little apart from the rest.

When they closed the coffin and were carrying it to the hearse, a woman from among the relatives sprang out onto the driveway, screaming. Four people had to hold her back. It was Audrey's mother, I knew, although I had never met her. She pulled those people with her, her arms stretched out to the coffin. But the coffin was too far, the space too wide. I felt a hotness in my eyes, filling up, filling up. I kept blinking to keep it back. Just because everyone was crying didn't mean I should cry. Nobody had seen me cry. Even now, I was the tough girl, I was tougher than most of them. I didn't want to break that image. As I looked at Audrey's mother, I felt so small, my concerns so stupid, my feelings so minute, because I could see what I felt was nothing.

When we got back on the bus, I passed Mrs. C., and she gave me a strange look. Her big eyes, magnified by her thick glasses, were red, and she had a wad of tissue in her hand. She was looking at my dry eyes, and I felt guilty. But Mrs. C., I wanted to say, it's not that I don't feel sad. Because Mrs. C., you only taught us equations and solutions, and I was supposed to know the solution to every problem. I was supposed to learn the ways to solve them, these theoretical numbers and signs and symbols put together. Just like I was supposed to be taught through imaginary lives what I was supposed to know about living and death, but again, I say to you, I am not interested in learning. I only want to learn how to get by, you know, flow along with the least amount of friction. Like flies maybe, I want to inhabit nice-smelling bushes and trees, and I didn't have to know what was creeping up on me with a big rolled-up newspaper. Because what makes us different from flies? We need air, we drown, and who cares if we get flushed down the toilet? Then I should have been able to look at you in the face, death with no capitals, because you don't mean anything, you only separate the conscious from the unconscious. But I couldn't look at Audrey. I knew that I couldn't want it enough to change it. I couldn't look at you because I didn't want life to be just that. A face in a box.

Haze Day

Jeffrey Lim

For many years now, as each planting season came, the slash-and-burn farmers of Indonesia would set alight huge swathes of rainforest to clear the land.

Sometimes, what was started as a controlled fire would blow into a raging inferno and send plumes of smoke into the air. With an easterly wind, the great black clouds would rise into the sky and drift towards neighbouring territories. Drift towards Singapore.

The day that Hwee Leng's father died, the local PSI reading hit 223. Meteorologists called it the worst bout of the Haze ever.

Thursday Night

Evan

Evan's neighbour's driveway spotlight was on again. Even though the venetians were as closed as he could get them, light still slipped through gaps and woke him.

He felt like an actor in one of those old movies where theyflashed a bright strip of light across his eyes.

When he proposed moving the bed, Amy complained that this would disrupt the fengshui. She told him to sleep on his back and not on his right side where he would face the window.

Easy for her to say, he thought. He'd been a side sleeper for all his life, so every night that began on his back ended unconsciously on his right, straight into the glare of those damn lights.

Amy wouldn't swap sides on their bed. "You know I always sleep on the left side. Go get yourself one of those eye masks."

"I can't sleep with an eye mask on," Evan had insisted. "It makes me uncomfortable."

"Oh, so now who's being inflexible?" Amy had retorted.

That was that.

When they bought thick drapes to block out the light, Amy had insisted instead on venetian blinds. A friend of hers had a shop at IMM where they had the colour she wanted. The only problem was that they were horrible, useless blinds. Light always managed to steal its way in. Amy refused to let him ask for his money back, owing to the need to maintain her friendship.

Evan got up, angry.

What was the neighbour doing?

Evan hated them. Well-heeled, smarmy know-it-all own-it-alls who stayed up late sampling wine, leaving the driveway lights on. Yuppies who probably had a rich mommy or daddy to make the down payment on their semi-detached house. He was disgusted with the way they went on their many holidays, asking Evan to look after their place while foisting Crabtree and Evelyn baskets to buy Amy's favour.

As for Evan himself, they had only paid off the mortgage on their home after thirty years of hard work. His retirement party had been at a cheap but good Chinese restaurant at Jalan Besar. They went up to Genting or Bintan for holidays. They thought that Johnson duck was the best thing since *bak chor mee*.

When it came down to it, Evan felt they did not deserve to live next to him.

He raised his hand in front of his face and turned the rod to open the blinds. Squinting through the cracks of his fingers, he could see the young man getting out of his car. He was dressed in some designer shirt, his face flushed with alcohol. The woman herself had made her way to the front door with a key, a scarf still wrapped around her arms.

Probably back from some yuppie function, Evan reasoned.

"Honey, shut the blinds," Amy said. Amy could bark an order even while half-asleep.

"Yes, dear," he muttered as he closed the blinds. He lay back onto the bed and stared up at the ceiling.

I'll fix them, he promised himself.

Fathul

Fathul eased the bus neatly into the bay. He squinted the sleep from his eyes. The doors opened with a long weary hiss.

Someone had spilt a sticky liquid under a seat in the upper deck. When Fathul returned with a mop, he noted that the passenger had also added to the graffiti that was previously there, scratched into the backing with a pen-knife.

"*Ai Wong loves Kenny*" was now complemented by "*but Kenny doesn't give a shit*".

Fathul plunged the head of the mop into his bucket and tried to ignore the smell.

Later that night, he returned to his three-room HDB flat and sloughed off the uniform shirt and slacks. When he had left them soaking in a porcelain sink full of cold water and some detergent, he sat at the foldable table in his kitchen and took out the cigarettes in his pants.

He imagined Rosianah telling him he shouldn't be smoking so late at night. He smiled to think of how she would shuffle about the flat in her slippers, the almost susurrous shhh-shhh of her feet as she dragged the plastic flats across the bare concrete, green plastic curlers in her hair.

Before she had fallen sick, she had been a restless woman,

utterly unable to sit still.

When he had finished his cigarette, Fathul would, as he always did every night after she had gone, lie down and gently stroke his hand over the space by his side.

Nallini

Nallini was unable to sleep. Tomorrow, she would try Valerie again.

The lawyers in the office never liked her, the gruff woman who made their tea.

Maybe they needed someone to clear the trash? Nallini was sure that, whatever they were charged by the cleaning contractor, they could save money if they gave her the job.

"I'm sorry," she kept hearing Valerie's voice in her head.

Valerie said a lot of things a month ago, but Nallini could only remember the word "sorry".

"I'll try to place a call for you to other firms," Valerie said, uncomfortably. "I'm sure we can get a place somewhere else for you."

Two tea ladies were unnecessary, she said. The managing partner had explained the situation to her in a letter which Valerie had passed to Nallini in a white unmarked envelope. They needed to cut costs. The secretaries had gossiped about when Nallini would be fired. They didn't know she understood Chinese.

"I heard they want to make one secretary work for two lawyers."

"Aiya, how to cope?"

"What to do? Hope they keep the ones who have been here longer."

"They should let the young ones go. They don't have families to worry about."

Nallini had just poured the boiled water into the spare pitcher and said nothing.

Now, with the last day of her notice about to start and with Valerie telling her that they could not find her any place in another firm, Nallini was tired. She was tired of thinking about how to spend less and thinking about how long her savings would last.

Maybe, she thought, they would agree to terminate the cleaning contractor. *Who could say no to a tea lady who also did the cleaning for the same price?*

Her lips were drawn into a thin line as she turned over on her side.

Hwee Leng

Hwee Leng woke suddenly.

It was 4.39 A.M. The early morning air made her shiver. She was sure that there was a reason why she had stirred from sleep. She leaned over to the bedside table and fumbled for the handphone.

The blue light of the phone hurt her eyes.

"1 Missed Call."

She gasped, feeling as though someone had squeezed her heart. She thumbed the button over the "Details" prompt, and, sure enough, Ah Tiong's number appeared. The "Time of Call" said she woke just a minute after the call had ended.

She found Ah Tiong's number and pressed it. As it rang, she drew her knees to her chest and tried not think about what he was going to tell her.

She wanted to hear the loud electronic whistle of a "No Answer" prompt. She wanted to hear Ah Tiong's recorded message asking her to call back or leave a message. She wanted to go back to sleep, thinking nothing had happened.

Instead, Ah Tiong's voice came on a pause when the ringing tone ended abruptly.

"Hello? Ah Leng?"

He sounded tired.

"How?" she asked.

"The doctor says you should come down. Can happen any time." There was a long pause, but Ah Tiong knew better than to prompt her.

"Okay," Hwee Leng said, her voice strangely flat. "I come now."

She found herself curiously numb as she got up and walked over to the toilet. The water felt cold across her face, but she seemed no more awake than she had already been.

As she dressed stoically by her window, she looked out over her estate at the long fluorescent-lit corridors of the neighbouring blocks. She used to think about how close each of the adjoining units had been and how she felt as though she had no privacy.

Now, all she could think was how distant this quiet, sleeping world looked.

The Cash Crop

A few days ago, a number of neighbouring slash-and-burn farmers (who had no idea that they were living near a drug kingpin's estate) were desperate to expand their meagre fields of tapioca and inadvertently set alight roughly four hundred hectares of one of Indonesia's underground marijuana production outfits.

Mr Wiyono Sutanto, the head of the underground organisation was unable to attend to these matters, because he was busy cowering under a hail of machine gun fire as his trusted lieutenant, Mr Harry Wirdoyono, attempted to seize control of Mr Sutanto's empire. The gun battle was destined to rage for the better part of the day, and each man's respective henchmen were too busy with each other to realise that the very produce they duelled over was going up in huge plumes of grey smoke.

Eventually, the battle resolved itself and Mr Sutanto's body was unceremoniously burned while Mr Wirdoyono's men gathered around their new boss.

First things were first, Mr Wirdoyono said. *Someone should put out the fires and take care of the farmers, show them that he was not to be trifled with.*

By the time the orders went out, more than two thirds of the cash crop was up in the air, making its way towards Singapore.

That was, as stated before, a few days ago.

Friday Morning

Fathul

The amber of the traffic lights at the junction of Bras Basah Road and Nicoll Highway were blinking with the rhythm of a heartbeat. Fathul gripped the steering wheel and swallowed. The acrid smoke managed to get in through the vents of his bus every time someone boarded.

There was something about the haze too. The smell was awful. It smelt faintly like a strange mix of plastic and herbs burning together. It made him nauseous.

He looked up at the traffic light. Fathul placed his hand on his chest.

He was fascinated. *The light is flashing to the beat of my heart . . .* he thought.

Casually, Fathul glanced up at the giant LCD screen high above the junction, the one mounted on the second and third floor, staring down at the junction of Nicoll Highway and Raffles Boulevard.

Fathul's head tilted to one side as colours raced across the screen.

As a mobile phone advertisement flashed across the screen, the images became an incomprehensible flow of lights and colours.

Fathul smiled and did not notice that other drivers had also stopped to look, each one of them oblivious to the tailback that was now stretching beyond the Rochor Flyover.

Nallini

Nallini made her way from the bus stop at Clifford Pier and over the bridge, on her way to Republic Plaza. Not knowing why, her usually brisk walk seemed to take forever.

She grew anxious as she made her way down the escalator at Caltex House. By the time she was walking past Change Alley, she was wobbling. This might have been alarming except that *everyone* else seemed to be doing the same.

All around her, men in ties and shirts lurched about, some pirouetting in the effort to stay on their feet. Women, formally dressed in their office clothes, were unable to address the task of stepping out in high heels. Some lost their balance, embracing the floor, arms splayed out in the fall. She saw at least a dozen collisions between individuals, and dozens more between pedestrian and building pillars, dustbins, lamp posts. As people dropped their papers, briefcases, handbags, Raffles Place MRT quadrangle became one large litter-fest.

Somehow, she made it to the office. Once there, she proceeded unsteadily to Valerie's office. She rapped on the door, but Valerie was asleep, head resting on her folded arms which lay on the table.

Nallini woke her and started speaking very slowly, pulling out the rehearsed speech she had worked on,

"Hi Miss Valerie, maybe I can help clean the toilets also ..."

She felt that her words were coming out of her mouth too slowly. Valerie herself was staring at Nallini's mouth, as if anticipating every word that Nallini managed to squeeze out. Her clumsy diction and tired mind laboured to complete a sentence.

Valerie suddenly smiled.

"Congra ... Congraaaaatuuuulayyyyyshunsss ... " Valerie replied. "Here ... your cheque ..."

Nallini sat down with her hands in her lap, the severance cheque clasped in her palms.

Then, forgetting that she had just been laid off, Nallini rose to her feet and stumbled over to the pantry to get the condensed milk, boiled water, tea, and coffee ready.

Evan

Evan had got up early. Amy had left for her morning brisk walk and he had been in his favourite spot on the porch with a paper.

The air was quite bad that morning. Still, he thought, it would not be long before the neighbours were gone.

Sure enough, the young couple managed to get out of the house, rushing, no doubt, because they were late.

No one, not Evan and not the couple, flinched or batted an eyelid as the car reversed a couple of times into their closed gate. Then, there was a click sound as one of the passengers in the Lexus remembered that the gate was still shut. The damaged driveway doors wobbled open with a loud and ugly whine.

The Lexus, rear fender severely dented, lurched out of the driveway and promptly reversed into a parked car on the opposite kerb. Rattled by the collision, his neighbours collected themselves and drove off, noisily scraping and damaging every other car parked along the kerb, their battered Lexus limping its way to the main street.

They had left their front door opened.

Evan, unable to resist himself, smiled.

Hwee Leng

Everybody's so strange today, Hwee Leng thought as she walked unsteadily to the hospital lift lobby.

She put out a hand to rest and balance herself and inadvertently hit the up button. The elevator chimed and she got in.

Her father was in a C ward. Four patients to a room, privacy was a curtain drawn round the bed.

Hwee Leng made her way round the corridors from the

elevators and walked past the reception counter where she saw two nurses snoring fitfully.

As she made her way to her father's room, she realised that the haze had come in through the windows in the corridors, and a thin film of the smoke filled the air. Vaguely perturbed, she looked for a nurse and found one who was seated on a chair looking down at her shoes.

"Miss? Shouldn't you close the windows?" she meant to say. Instead, Hwee Leng could hear herself make unintelligible words. When the nurse did not answer, Hwee Leng leaned forward and saw that she was fast asleep.

She made her way to her father's room. Ah Tiong was there already. Her father was awake. The windows were thrown wide open. The other patients in the room were either asleep or staring ahead, as if watching invisible shapes.

Friday Afternoon

Nallini

Nallini was standing before the pantry counter. She had tucked the severance cheque into the back pocket of her trousers. Now, with as much speed as she could muster (which was not much), she cleaned the cups, brewed the coffee, and set the tea bags.

A small line of secretaries had formed up behind her (in slow motion) an hour ago. A few had fallen asleep and were lying on the office carpet, dozing. A few had managed to cover up the gaps in the line by stepping over their fallen colleagues.

The first in line was Madam Ho, the managing director's secretary. Madam Ho was usually early in the pantry. She was also the loudest. No one dared to offend her because of her boss.

"Eh," Madam Ho said blinking heavily. "Why didn't you collect my boss's cup from his room this morning?" Stumbling, she shoved the unwashed mug at Nallini.

"Don't think you can take it easy just because it's your last day," Madam Ho managed to say. She leaned against the wall and closed her eyes. "Ai . . ." she sighed, "so sleepy today . . . Don't forget ah, three teaspoons of . . . condensed . . . milk . . ." She closed her eyes, and seemed to drift.

Nallini nodded obediently and turned to open the cabinet to look for the condensed milk. Unfortunately, she found herself spending an inordinate amount of time trying to decide which was the can of condensed milk and which was the white milky bottle of milk of magnesia.

Conscious of how time was flying by, Nallini had to make a snap decision.

Evan

He sighed with satisfaction. Even his neighbour's dog, a Schnauzer, was sedated. The little monster was asleep where it would usually be barking away at Evan if he so much as came within a foot of the house gates. Now, Evan was standing over its sleeping form in the neighbour's living room.

He found a pair of scissors on the living room coffee table and staggered back to its sleeping form. It lay there limply in his arms as he proceeded to gather its fur in little clumps and snipped away. A half hour or so later, Evan had finished and moved on to the kitchen.

He found the corkscrew and opened the wine cooler, reading the labels on each of the bottles carefully, delighting at how old and exotic each wine was. Here there was a South African Merlot, 1997. There, was a French Chardonnay from 1983. And oh look, there was a Wolf Blass Silver Label. It was a pity that Evan had given up drinking many years ago since it had become too expensive. Even he felt that it was a bit of a shame as he uncorked each bottle and poured its contents down the kitchen sink. Still, Evan imagined that he must have inhaled some of the fumes because he felt incredibly addled by the time he finished replacing each bottle back in its slot.

He reached the telephone and began going through the list of names there. Yes, there were all the international friends he expected this yuppie jet-setting couple to have. The list was full of wholly unpronounceable surnames described as living in distant countries.

Well, he reasoned, one *has* to start alphabetically. Each ring tone was followed by some irate person on the line invariably complaining about what time it was on the other side of the world.

Evan's message for them was always the same: "Hello, is Ah Long there? Ah Long from Singapore? Don't bluff, you are Ah Long . . . Eh? But you sound like Ah Long . . . Okay, maybe you're not Ah Long, but how about chatting a little?"

When he exhausted the phone book, Evan felt some satisfaction at having racked up probably more than a hundred overseas calls, most of which lasted a minute or so.

The expensive and fragile lace and dry-clean only clothes were a bit harder to stuff into the washing machine, but he managed, and he emptied the last of the bleach before putting the machine on for a heavy wash.

With the rumbling of the overloaded washing machine behind him, Evan staggered out of his neighbour's house, happy with the job he had done. He stood in the driveway, wondering whether he had forgotten anything.

After giving it some careful thought, he decided he had not left anything out and walked back to his house where he found Amy passed out on the living room floor in her exercise clothes, her sweat-soaked towel in one hand and an MP3 player clasped in another.

Fathul

Rosianah had loved the beach, especially Bedok jetty. Before she fell ill, they used to go there at night to catch fish. He remembered the small radio they'd strapped to their bicycle, together with the fishing tackle and the bait. She would pack *nasi lemak* for them, and bring two groundsheets, one which they laid out on the ground and the other which they tied to the railing to create a makeshift shelter in case of rain.

He smiled to think of how happy she was there.

When she fell ill, he bought a small motorcycle and drove her there until she had no more strength to hold on to his waist or to even walk.

He could see the sea now, the lazy waves lapping weakly at the litter-strewn shoreline.

The East Coast beach was an ugly beach. It was nothing like Perhentian or the beaches along the east coast of peninsular Malaysia.

The bus ground to a halt and he opened the doors.

Turning to the passengers behind him, he noticed many of them were asleep.

"Last stop!" he called.

He made his way through to the back of each deck, gently nudging each passenger awake and ushering them off his bus and then stepped out of the vehicle and locked the doors.

With the sun and wind on his face, he left the bus sinking into the sand and walked out onto the jetty, breathing in the hazy air deeply.

If any passenger had noticed that the bus had left Nicoll Highway and was at the beach, they might have said something. But no one mentioned a thing.

Hwee Leng

Her father was happy, she reasoned. He had said nothing, only smiled benignly at them as he passed away.

Ah Tiong had not said a word, merely smiled himself and said something about how her father had wanted the windows opened because the air soothed him.

"He's just being a smoker to the end," Ah Tiong had said. Hwee Leng could only laugh until the tears filled her eyes.

Friday Night

By Friday night, the haze began to clear up a little as a shower started.

On the road where Evan lived, an annoyed (and bald) Schnauzer awoke from its stupor and made its way to the door barking noisily. A battered Lexus was towed into the driveway. The owner of the car stumbled out of the tow truck, paid the vehicle driver, and switched on the lights in the house only to be greeted by his now hairless dog. He rushed, and stumbled out on to the driveway looking around for the vandal. Instead, he could only see a wrecked car lying under the driveway spotlight. At least the vandals hadn't broken any lights or taken any furniture.

As for Evan, the glare of the driveway lights that blared their way in through the venetians into his eyes became a rueful reminder that he had forgotten to take care of one small detail.

In Raffles Place, an Indian tea lady, now formally no longer employed, put up her umbrella as she emerged from a bank branch, having deposited her cheque, and made her slow and unsteady way to the MRT entrance. When she last left her office, there had been a queue outside the toilets.

In Bedok, a bus driver raised his hands to the sky and laughed as the water soaked his shirt through while his passengers sat in the sand and watched the clouds pass over the sea.

In a hospital, Hwee Leng and her brother made it out of the C-class ward and out to the bus stop, heads aching from the fumes. Still, although they were wet from the rain, and the bus was late, very late, Hwee Leng could only remember the wan smile on her father's face when he had died.

By Saturday midnight, the haze had lifted and the PSI had dropped back to a healthier 34.

The meteorologists called it the worst bout of the Haze ever. But there were more than a few who wished that it had stayed longer.

Thirteen Ways of Looking at a Hanging

Alfian bin Sa'at

1.

Ricky is summoned from his cell. They're going to take a few photos of him today, he's told. But they're not the usual mugshots—profile, front, deer in headlights. They're gifts. The Prison Department thinks that, as a gesture of their generosity, they will take photos of Ricky and send them to his family and friends. Is he to autograph them as well? Ricky doesn't know. All he knows is that this would be a break from his usual routine: waking up, breakfast, relieving himself, lunch, dinner, sleep. All in a cell measuring three square metres.

It will be a welcome change of scenery. To take the photos they will have to bring him to another area. Apparently, his cell does not provide the best setting for a photography session, with its greyish walls, a squat toilet, and a bucket. However, four days before the execution, the cell will undergo a minor redecoration: they will bring in a television set for him to watch. Ricky has heard that the set will be placed in a wire-frame pen, to prevent him from either damaging it or damaging himself.

Ricky is looking forward to that—perhaps the sound from the TV might finally be able to drown out the sound of his own thoughts. Wasn't that why he often switched the TV on when alone in hotel rooms—not so much to follow the programmes but to maintain a background of empty chatter? But how much distraction will it be able to provide him in his cell? He will be watching images flicker behind a metal grid, and he will never be able to forget, even momentarily, the fact that he is in prison. How can one do that while staring at a TV set blasting at you from inside its own cage?

Ricky sits up from his mat and smooths down the hair at the back of his head. He squats by his bucket, scoops up some water, and washes his face. He makes his way to the half-open door, where a guard is waiting. Ricky remembers being told by one of the wardens that they'll take thirteen photos of him.

But why? What significance is there in that number? They had probably made their calculations and arrived at thirteen: the average number of relatives and close friends for a typical death row prisoner. A figure arrived at after subtractions, taking into account those who are estranged, who have given up or decided that what they consider their social circle should not include condemned inmates. Thirteen: the maximum number of facial expressions that a human face possesses. Thirteen: the number of photographs a photographer could take before the monstrosity of the routine taps his conscience and paralyses him.

Thirteen. The guard looks at Ricky. "Handsome, how? We're taking your pictures today." Ricky pulls the front of his T-shirt and wipes his face with it.

"I know," he says.

2.

One of these days, Ricky will have to be weighed. The method of execution that has been prescribed for him is hanging, by the long-drop method. Certain calculations have to be performed so that the force of gravity acting on his body will cause an instantaneous death.

After Ricky's weight has been noted, a rehearsal will be performed with a sandbag of equal weight. This is to determine the length of the "drop". If the rope is too long, he might be decapitated; if it is too short, death by strangulation could take as long as forty-five minutes.

The rope also has to undergo some strict specifications. It should be 1.9 cm to 3.2 cm in diameter, boiled and stretched to "eliminate spring or coiling". The knot should be lubricated with wax or soap "to ensure a smooth sliding action".

Immediately before the execution, his hands and legs will be tied, and he will be blindfolded, either with a strip of cloth around the eyes or a cloth bag over the head. The noose will be placed around his neck, with the knot behind the left ear. A trapdoor is then opened, and he will fall through. His weight should cause a quick fracture-dislocation of the neck. However, cases of instantaneous death are rare.

The fracture-dislocation fails to be immediate in the event of the following: if Ricky is very light, has strong neck muscles, if the "drop" is too short, or the noose has been wrongly positioned. Death will then result from slow asphyxiation.

If this occurs, Ricky's face will become bluish and engorged, his tongue will protrude, and his eyes will pop. In addition, he may defecate while suspended, and his limbs may move spasmodically and violently.

3.

Other than the cell, the only area that Ricky has been to is the exercise yard, where he gets to stretch his legs and jog around for half an hour each day. Sometimes he does this alone, and sometimes another prisoner from a different isolation cell gets to join him. Ricky usually doesn't have much to say to the other guy. They'd acknowledge each other with a smile, or a nod, and then settle into their respective routines. For Ricky, this would be a series of stretches, squats, push-ups, and dips at the bench. Sometimes the other guy would also have his own exercise routine, but somehow careful not to be doing the same things as Ricky, for the self-conscious fear of being seen as either a copycat or a competitor.

One day though, a thought flashed across Ricky's mind: *we're both going to die soon, and here we are keeping our bodies fit.* As the session wore on, Ricky realised how desperately he wanted to share this insight with the other guy, though he wasn't sure whether it was something that would come out as a morbid joke or an indignant rant. Maybe he would know only as he spoke the words, and saw their real meaning spread across the other guy's face. But how could he even broach it? Wouldn't he have to make some small talk first? A line like that, however urgent and profound it seemed to Ricky at that time, was not a conventional ice-breaker.

Ricky tried to catch the other guy's attention, but the latter seemed completely absorbed pacing up and down the length of the exercise yard. It would have made more sense to call the yard a very large room, since it was completely enclosed and windowless. One couldn't see the sky at all, much less any greenery. Did it make the ones who ran the prison feel any better by giving it that name? Or were the prisoners themselves supposed to indulge in the illusion too, imagining for themselves the freedom a term like "yard" is supposed to conjure?

The other guy was looking down at his feet as he paced. It was almost as if he was counting his footsteps, first in one direction, and then the other, to make sure the figures tallied. Ricky looked at him, his brows furrowed, and he attempted telepathy. *Look at me. There's something I have to tell you.* A glance, some acknowledgement, would be the sign for Ricky to approach him. But the other guy was oblivious, protected by his solitude. Before he knew it, the half hour was up. Ricky felt the words he wanted to say turn into something solid, lodged like a clot in his heart.

4.

The older of two brothers. Father ran a business. Mother was a housewife. Wanted to be a pilot. But eyes weren't good. Grades weren't good either. Went to study in Australia. Ended up working for his father. Family business. Had smoked pot while overseas. Went back, and on a whim, started asking around. Finally managed to score pot. Was introduced to heroin during a session. Hooked. Started dealing. Bags into straws. Narcotics raid. Identified as owner of rental flat where more than fifteen grammes of heroin was found. Sentenced to death.

5.

Ricky is handcuffed. He is told to follow the guard, who leads him along corridors and staircases. Another guard tails them from behind. The guard in front rifles through a set of keys each time he opens a door. At the final door though, he knocks.

A man in office attire opens it. He tells the guard that the photographer is arriving soon and that he is being cleared at the gates. The air-conditioned room is furnished with a table, a swivel chair, and shelves of books and ring files. There is a laminated poster on the wall, with a picture of a hang glider sweeping over a canyon and the word "Inspiration" in capital letters.

The man who opened the door passes Ricky a set of attire, consisting of a white shirt, grey pants, a black-and-maroon striped necktie and a belt. Whoever put the ensemble together had a sense of humour.

"I have to put on the tie?" Ricky asks.

"If you don't know how to do, I can tie for you," the man who opened the door replies.

Ricky knows how to knot a tie. But the idea of putting a tie on someone who is sentenced to hang strikes him as somewhat bizarre. Is he reading too much into it? Or are these people simply unaware of these unfortunate resonances? Ricky peels off his T-shirt and slips into the white shirt. The starched feel of the fabric against his skin makes him wince; it reminds him of the times when he went into heroin withdrawal. The slightest contact with his own clothes had then felt like he was being scoured by steel wool.

After fastening the last button, Ricky immediately feels that he has soiled the shirt. He had washed himself in the morning, but during the course of the afternoon had perspired as he lay on his mat. Who do these clothes belong to? Or are they specially set aside for these photo sessions? Will he leave pit stains on it? His body's smell? Ricky decides that these are just costumes, props. Nobody will want to wear these clothes, which are no longer just fabric, but which now serve, after repeated fittings, as the collective aura of a series of doomed figures. They will be passed down from one transient body to another, the men having served their time—a few precious minutes of illusion—in them.

He wears the pants over his prison shorts. He feels that, by doing so, he manages to resist participating wholeheartedly in this charade. After putting on his belt, Ricky scans the room for a pair of shoes. The man in office attire seems to have read his mind. He produces a pair of black shoes from behind the desk, along with socks. They are at least two sizes too big for Ricky, but he puts them on anyway. Ricky strings the tie around his neck and makes a knot, expertly. He pulls it up until he can feel the pressure on his carotids. Then he loosens it and turns down his collars.

6.

Other than his cell and exercise yard, the only other area Ricky has been to is the visiting booth, where he gets to talk to his visitors through a telephone, separated by a thick pane of glass. He receives visitors once a week, for twenty minutes each time.

It is usually his mother and brother who come to visit. They tell him that his father is ill, but Ricky doesn't believe them. "Addicts never change," his father had once told him, and sometimes Ricky had felt as if this was not so much a final sigh of disappointment but a savage curse placed on him. How else could he respond to something like that other than by ultimately proving that his father was right?

Ricky sometimes wished he had something more to say to his mother and brother. If only he could leave them with a set of instructions, a verbal will, the things that would need tending in his absence. But he had no attachments, no dependants, nothing that required an irreplaceable touch. No heirloom, no plants to water, nothing in his bank account. All the things that had perhaps once mattered to him: an SLR camera, designer clothes, a motorcycle, had all been sold off to feed his habit. At one point of time he had even laughed when he was told the life he was leading was one of excess; he could not think of anything more ascetic than forgoing rounds of drinks, a haircut, even meals, for a puff of smoke.

His mother would usually start the conversation, with the boy sitting by her side. He was seventeen, and sometimes Ricky felt that he tagged along because there was a cautionary, moral lesson to be witnessed. At times Ricky would feel as if he was something in an aquarium, his features distorted, dappled with unearthly shadows, his speech as inconsequential as a stream of bubbles.

Ricky's cynicism often doesn't last, and within a minute into the visit he would realise that there is no point in mentally interrogating the motives of the people at the other side of the glass. "Have you eaten?" his mother would begin. "What did you eat today?" Ricky would describe to her what he had for lunch, and resist the temptation to tell her that he misses her food. The last time he did that, she had broken down and could not stop crying for five minutes.

Cooking, in his family, was contact. They were not used

to physical expressions of affection, and the only time Ricky remembered hugging his parents was at the airport, when he took his first plane to Australia, about to embark on his university studies. Even then, the hugs were awkward, his mother patting his back and uttering "mmm, mmm", his father, bony, unaccustomed, but nevertheless obliging, allowing Ricky for the first time in his life to receive a whiff of what his father smelt like—a sensation which both repulsed him and filled him with tenderness.

And then his mother would go on, describing the rest of the family: his father, too ill to leave the house, his aunt, the one who's diabetic and puffing up from steroids, an uncle having an affair with a China mistress. Ricky would listen, his hand on the telephone, smiling or frowning on cue, but most of the time he would be tuning in to the texture of his mother's voice, not its contents: its inflections, the sigh at the end of sentences, the fragile laughter. He would never tell her this, but it is the voice that he wants to imagine, if it is at all within his control, at the hour of his death.

When it came to the brother's turn, it was Ricky who did most of the talking. The brother was still in the army, and so could only visit on weekends. Ricky felt sorry for him; he knew most army boys would rather spend their precious weekends trying to compensate for all the deprivations they had endured in camp. Because of this, Ricky did not expect him to be very communicative; in fact, he often looked a little sulky, never looking at Ricky straight in the eyes, his shoulders stooped with reluctance. Thus Ricky would ask about his life in camp and once joked how he felt that prison food was still better than the stuff they served in the army.

When it was time to leave, Ricky observed how his mother's eyes would unfailingly well up with tears. Ricky ended every visit by saying, "Ma, I have to go." He often wondered what effect these words had on her; for him they were the only things he wanted to say. Everything else was just spoken for the sake of reassuring his visitors that he was capable of banal conversation, of recalling events and reminiscing trivia, to demonstrate that his present situation has not driven him mad. Or maybe that was the way he maintained sanity, by distilling the unspeakable to four words, spoken with equanimity and with a desire to comfort: "I have to go".

After the departure of his mother and brother, Ricky would retire to his cell, and self-pity would consume him. He could imagine his mother telling the boy, after making their way out of the prison complex, both of them squinting in the sunlight: *Don't ever be like him, don't ever break my heart like him.* But Ricky was often wrong. It was much more likely for the mother to ask, "Do you think he's lost weight? He looked so thin just now." And the brother would answer that Ricky had not, that she shouldn't worry, while secretly wondering if it was possible for someone to lose so much weight as to confound any attempt to hang him.

7.

The clerk looked at the identity card in her hand.

> Name: Ricky Lam Wai Mun (Lin Weiwen)
> Race: Chinese
> Date of Birth: 18-07-1977
> Sex: M
> Country of Birth: Singapore
> Date of Issue: 02-08-1993
> Address: Blk 542, Hougang Street 21, #09-17, S(309542)
> Blood type: O+

After receiving the coroner's report, she will punch a hole in the card. She usually finds a space in the corner for the hole, avoiding the photograph and the thumbprint. She will then slip the card and a letter from the prison to the family of the deceased. It is not a condolence letter, but one that will inform the family to collect the body of the deceased within twenty-four hours. The clerk did not type the letter herself. She had inherited it from her predecessors. She did not see any need to revise it; it says what it needs to say. *You are hereby informed.* The letter is usually sent out by Friday afternoon, a few hours after the dawn hangings. It arrives on Monday.

The clerk contemplated the photo on the card. "He's quite good looking," she thought. Large eyes, spiky hair, sharp cheekbones, a broad, sturdy neck. There was also something candid about the expression, as if the subject had not wanted to have his photo taken, and would have scowled in protest a few seconds later. It was a face on the brink of saying something. *I'm not ready yet.* And then the camera flashed.

A Cantonese boy, the clerk thought, judging from the name. And so young too. "Wasted," she thought. "So wasted."

8.

The man in office attire hands Ricky a jacket. It is black, and the tailoring looks a bit shabby.

"Up to you whether you want to wear or not," the man says.

Ricky suddenly feels an almost dizzying fatigue sweep across him. Why is he being dressed up in this manner? Why can't he just pose inside his cell with his white T-shirt and blue shorts? What is the purpose of this elaborate artifice?

It strikes Ricky that the photos are not supposed to be mementoes for himself—they are, rather, keepsakes meant for those close to him. But wouldn't these people already own photos of Ricky? Did the prison think that it was providing some kind of service for those who had never possessed cameras?

Perhaps the intention was to recommend a recent photograph for potential use in an obituary, or for funeral display. And of course they would not want such a picture to show the subject in prison garb. The clothes had to be generic, but why not something a bit more casual? Ricky cannot remember the last time he had put on a jacket.

The most plausible explanation that Ricky can think of is that these costumes were not chosen for how much they reflected a certain ground reality, but for their aspirational reach. The prison probably believed the ideal life for anyone is that of a suit in an office, a managerial position perhaps, complete with a desktop computer and family photos on a shelf.

But it is not the kind of life that Ricky has ever considered for himself. To pose in these clothes is to subscribe to a fantasy dreamed up by bureaucrats with limited imaginations. It is to join in the valorisation of smug, self-consoling white-collar values, while admitting, with a touch of remorse, how far one has strayed from them.

Ricky hands the jacket back to the man. The man suggests that Ricky wear it for some of the shots, for "variety". Ricky is not persuaded.

9.

Once, a few days after the abortive counter with the footstep-counting guy, Ricky had been allowed sole use of the yard. As he was doing his push-ups, he suddenly thought about the indignity of being provided with a roaming zone. As zoos evolved, animals were transferred from cages to landscaped enclosures. This was because it was inhumane to restrict their natural instincts for movement, for space. The yard existed simply because the prison did not want to be accused of mistreatment. Exercise was a right that any human being was entitled to. But Ricky did not feel like a human being, he felt like an animal. He was a hamster, pleasing its master by scurrying inside a hamster wheel.

So Ricky turned around and lay on his back. He stretched his legs and laid his hands on his chest. He closed his eyes. He would choose to exercise his freedom by keeping still. The guard asked if he was all right.

"You need to see the doctor?"

"I'm fine," said Ricky. He was conducting an experiment: was there any difference between lying down on a three-square-metre cell and in a large room? He once had a girlfriend who attended yoga lessons, who would tell him about the fields of energy that spaces contain. Could he feel any now? He tried a visualisation exercise: how far was his body from the nearest wall, how far was that wall from other walls, where did the walls end? He thought about the absurd thought that had seized him a few days ago and which he eventually buried inside him, having lost the opportunity to tell someone. Was it possible to eject the thought now, like an invisible spray, into the room? Maybe in the future, someone will pick up the same thought, not realising that it was Ricky who had originated it. This man who laid down on the floor one day and sent it out from the depths of his silence, like a halo. Staining the ceilings and walls with light. Ricky the psychic vandal.

The guard looked on, puzzled. Ricky was smiling.

10.

The photographer apologises for being late. He is probably in his late twenties, much like Ricky. He is a professional. He walks around the room, passing his name card to the two guards and the man in the office attire. He tells them that he also does bridal photography and has a studio of his own located at some industrial park.

Smoothly, the photographer sets up his tripod, positioning his camera on top of it. Ricky recognises the model.

"Is that a Nikon FM10?" he asks.

The photographer seems rather unsettled by Ricky's question.

"You into cameras?"

"I had one of those," Ricky replies. "But mine was second-hand."

The photographer isn't sure how to respond. He had never really engaged any of the inmates he photographed in conversation before. He glances at the guards, to see if there is anything out of the ordinary about the exchange, whether protocol has been transgressed. They are impassive, even bored.

"It's a good camera," is all the photographer can say. Ricky is then asked to stand behind the desk, against the bookshelves. "Just relax ah," the photographer says. "Don't be so stiff. And smile." Ricky refuses to smile. He stares straight at the camera's lens, projecting what he believes to be a blank expression. He had already decided on this a few days ago; he would subtract all possible emotion from his face. He would allow its features to submit to a loss of muscle tone—he imagined his eyes going dim, his jowls slackening. The only discernible expression on his face will be tiredness.

"Sorry," the photographer says. "Can smile?"

Ricky does not comply. For a moment, he is afraid that the camera will capture a steely defiance on his face, rather than the effacement, the retreat he is trying so hard to achieve, his visage existing in a plane posterior to his borrowed clothes. Ricky blinks, and his face does not change.

"Ricky, you trying to be funny or what?" one of the guards asked.

"I can't smile, sir," Ricky says, his voice flat and emotionless.

11.

One day, during a visit, a girl accompanies his mother and brother. She is introduced as his brother's wife. She is very young, probably in her late teens. His mother tells her to talk to Ricky first. Realising that there is not much time for an exchange of pleasantries, Ricky asks the first question that is on his mind.

"My brother's still in the army. Don't you think you're both too young to get married?"

The girl smiles shyly. And then she tells Ricky, "You're going to be an uncle."

Ricky is stunned. It's a shotgun wedding, he thinks. But at the same time, a feeling of what could only be described as joy spreads through him. He looks at his brother, who bears an expression of both chastisement and pride.

"How many months now?"

"Five."

"Can you feel him kicking already?"

"Yah."

Ricky feels like reaching out through the glass, to place a hand on the girl's belly. He doesn't mind not being able to hug his visitors or to wipe away the tears from his mother's face; all he wants is to just rest his hand on the bump of this girl who he's met for the first time. Ricky's brother is next on the phone.

"*Kor*, why are you crying? You never cried before."

"Congratulations, man."

"Army pay not enough ah, *kor*."

"You'll survive."

"We decided to keep the baby." And then Ricky's brother said, in a deliberate manner, almost as if for the benefit of whoever was eavesdropping on their conversation, "Actually this kind of thing not for us to decide one. How can we anyhow kill the baby?"

"You'll be a good father."

"Aiyah, only you say."

"It's a dying man's words. You better believe it, okay?"

The words had rushed out ahead of Ricky. All this time they had been avoiding the topic of his execution: Ricky, for fear of losing control and transforming each session into outpourings of naked grief, and his visitors, for fear of damaging Ricky's morale, or worse, nurturing false hopes. For the rest of the visit, this particular family, strangely resistant for so long, finally succumbed to the helplessness often witnessed in the visitor's area. They pressed their palms against the smeared, non-conducting glass, choked on their sobs, and did not leave even after the bell was rung. A simple tactic was employed to usher them away: the guards simply switched off all the lights.

12.

The photographer has already taken eleven photographs. Ricky has been made to pose standing up, sitting behind the desk, holding a pen, and once, after some friendly entreaties from the photographer, while wearing the black jacket. In each of the photographs, Ricky's face is aloof and vacant.

There are only two shots left. It has been the most trying session the photographer has ever conducted. The subject is uncooperative and somehow immune to his jokes. One of the consolations that he's supplied for this particular task is that he believes his camera flash is able to banish the shadow of death cast over the faces of his subjects. For a moment, they appear alive, their faces brimming with expectation.

"You have two shots left," the photographer said. "Are you sure you still don't want to smile?"

Ricky shakes his head. He knows he is in control of this photo session. He can sense everyone in the room getting uncomfortable by his refusal to treat the session as a privilege, to display the necessary gratitude. He wants them to realise the perversity of this well-intentioned ritual—if his mother were to receive one of these photos, what is she supposed to think? That his time in prison was never as bad as she had imagined, since here was proof that inmates were allowed to participate in role-playing excursions, flights of fancy that transported them from their implacable fate? That, despite all the mortifications he has been subjected to, the prison recognised his essential humanity and permitted its singular expression during a photo shoot?

No. The photos, all thirteen, would strike her as testimonies of regret: *what could have been*. Here is your son; this is what he would have turned out to be if he had not dabbled in drugs. This is the son that every mother would have wanted: the smart clothes, his own office, the proud smile. *A life like this is within everyone's reach, the problem with your son is that he chose to reject it.* The law is a line separating binaries: there is normality, and there is crime. There is the office, and there are the gallows. The sum of your son's life: a roll of undeveloped negatives.

The photographer takes another shot. Ricky still refuses to smile. "This is the last one," the photographer sighs. "It's your last chance. Try to smile, okay? Don't do it for me. Do it for your parents, your girlfriend, whoever. Don't you want to be remembered?"

13.

Ricky is back in his cell. He is lying on his side, facing the wall, and crying. For the final shot, he had capitulated; it had something to do with the photographer saying the words, "last chance".

At that moment, he ceased to be concerned with his smile as a symbol, a mark on his face to be deciphered. Smiling, for him, became an exercise of will, the body's ability to resist the effects of gravity, lifting his features, for an instant, above the long drop, the abyss. His eyes began filling with tears as he strained to push the sides of his mouth upwards, looking desperately at the camera, almost begging it to capture whatever was left of his soul.

The Drowning

Dave Chua

When they hear about the tsunami, they do not make the connection. Only when he gets home does he realise that something is wrong. He turns to her.

"Where did Thomas say that he went?" he says.

"Was it China? Hangzhou?" She replies. Her attention is divided between the Korean drama serial and dinner, but now she is fully alert.

"Check the e-mail?" he asks.

She puts down her chopsticks and rushes over to turn on the computer; she searches for the switch desperately. He gets up and points it out to her. He smells the perfume she has put on. The computer starts up slowly, and they watch the screen change and turn.

He clicks open the e-mail programme and opens the last e-mail he has sent. Chan racks his brain trying to remember. Surely it has to be China. Thomas said that he wanted to go to Shanghai.

"Ma, I will be at Phuket," the e-mail reads. Chan's heart sinks. Then they are on the phone and calling whoever they can: the High Commission, the Embassy. There are trails of phone numbers, of kind voices struggling to make sense of a disaster that did not even happen here.

"Can you tell me if he is safe?" Mrs. Chan shrieks.

The Drowning

But no one can. On the news, serious-faced reporters are at the various locations ravaged by the disaster and commenting on the number dead. Chan flips through the channels. None of them talks about Phuket for more than two minutes. The footages they have show a city in darkness.

"Do we have any of his friends' phone numbers?" Mrs. Chan asks.

They dig out old numbers and call, but none of them has been in touch with him.

"Does he have a roommate?" Mrs. Chan asks.

But the only number they have is his mobile. They leave their dinner to grow cold on the table and get a taxi. The taxi driver senses their urgency and comforts them. "It is probably nothing." He takes out a piece of folded yellow paper and passes it to Mr. Chan. "For his safety," he says.

They go to the door and knock, but there is no one home. They ask the neighbours if they know, but the Indian man next door has never spoken to him. Mr. Chan wants to get a locksmith to open the door. He tells Mrs. Chan to go home. He throws his body against the door a few times. The neighbour comes out to stare but does not help.

She keeps dialling and calling. She must have called his number a hundred times, and he tells her that Thomas's phone may not be able to get any reception.

In the morning, they sit outside the door, but it is still unopened. Mrs. Chan falls asleep on the brown matted rug next to the shoe rack. Chan tears up the piece of yellow paper. When the office opens, he calls his travel agent and books the tickets to fly in the afternoon. But the airlines have cancelled their flights for the next few days. The sun is pouring on his face, and he calls work to tell them that he is not coming in. His boss scolds him for about five minutes, and, when Mr. Chan does not reply, his boss realises that something is wrong. Chan speaks about his son, and his boss tells Chan to take all the time he needs; he has too much leave anyway from previous years.

They leave the apartment and return home to pack after securing a flight out. The airplane is empty. Are they the only passengers on board? Mr. Chan watches the corrugated surface of the sea from his seat. The sun is sparkling on the waters. He expects to see a figure waving back at him. His son with sunglasses, trying to tell them that he is all right.

They land at the airport, and all around them are aid workers and those waiting for their airplanes to land and take them away, like overstayers at a party now desperate to leave. They carry their bottles of mineral water, and his wife's handbag and suitcase are jammed full of biscuits. Food might be difficult to find.

They stumble to an aid centre and enter their plea. Mrs. Chan is prepared. She has called up one of her former students and made photocopies of wanted posters for her son. The lady at the stall did not charge a cent for them. She might not have children, but she knew her pain, she said.

They want the driver to go to the beach. They do not speak Thai and rely on hand signals to communicate. The driver wants more baht. He does not take off his sunglasses. His hand signals claim that his children were washed away as well. Mr. Chan asks how he can work? The driver shouts what can he do? He tosses the baht at the driver. Who can care about money now?

When they arrive at the beach, they see that the damage is great. Fences have been smashed. Statues tossed to the side. There is a Garuda with a cracked beak, its eyes imploring skyward.

They venture to the crisis centre where a mob is gathering. There is much shrieking and screaming. An old man is beating his chest hard. Three children play with a golf ball. Chickens scream randomly even though it is noon.

"Where do we start?" Mr. Chan says. He goes around asking

the staff. He queues up, not knowing what the queues are for.

Even his creation appeared mechanical and necessary, guided by his parents and social norms. When he was born, they were grateful. He was unflawed, perfect. Chan had thought that their charade of a marriage would breed a monster, a creature so maligned that they would be branded and thrown out. Mr. Chan felt redeemed. They decided to stay together for his sake. But their son knew that theirs was a loveless marriage. When he was in junior college, he started to give tuition and working as a lifeguard on weekends. It kept him out of the house, and they only saw him briefly. There was never any reason for the Chans to protest their son's constant exile from the flat. Conversations at dinner were sparse and muted. Chan knew that this was the flow of life. That someone who had trusted him so completely and been so eager to tell everything he learnt and the secrets of his schoolmates and teachers would quietly close up into himself.

The first chance he could get, he moved out. Even when he was in the army, he liked to stay out, away from home.

After he completed his National Service, he stayed in the university dorms, which suited his lifestyle more. Mr. Chan did not fight the decision. He did not have the will or strength to fight his own son. He could have done anything, and Chan would not have raised his hand. He grew up smart and strong, not at the top of his class but in the upper middle of his pack. Good enough to get into a local university.

He went to work at an accounting firm and soon had a big desk with a plaque bearing his name. They had a photo of that. His son wearing his red and yellow striped tie, smiling at the camera, pointing at the lens, the background a muddy orange-yellow.

They show whoever they can the pictures, but nobody has seen him. His wife wants to do a version of the poster in Thai. They need to get a local mobile phone. There are just too many people missing. Soon, the man at the counter asks if they have checked the hospital. They reply no, and the man, his nails dirty with ink, tells them to take a cab and see if their son is there.

They go to the hospital, where entire corridors are draped with dead bodies and covered with white sheets. Dry ice has been heaped around to keep the bodies cool, and it feels like they have entered one of the outer layers of Hell as they walk amongst the dead, looking for their son. Even with the cold, the bodies have started to rot, and the sweet smell makes Chan want to choke. But he steadies himself against the wall and walks amongst the dead. He stops over the corpse of one man whose mouth is barely open. He has a cloth bracelet around his wrist.

"Why are we here? This is not him," she says. She continues to walk amongst the corpses, a blue and white checker handkerchief over her mouth.

After the second batch, he has to slow down as he inspects every dead face. He can hear sobbing break out and occasional screams. There are guavas and incense ashes on the floor. The smoke from joss sticks and ice makes it feel like they have walked into one of the rooms of the afterlife.

But they do not see him. The aide asks if they want to see the children.

"How big are they?"

"About half your height," the aide says.

"No. They can't be him," Chan replies.

"There are more bodies coming. Maybe you come tomorrow," the aide says. Chan turns to him with a tired look and is not sure that he can face so many corpses again.

The Drowning

The hotel they are in has been spared from damage. There are children playing in the street and stray dogs with beggar eyes barking for scraps.

"He must be somewhere," she says.

Chan calls his mobile number a few more times. Maybe this is all in error. But still no one answers.

Chan tells her to go to sleep. The moon is out, and the honking of cars makes it hard for him to close his eyes. He feels that the street below must be full of ghosts, but there are only scooter riders and wild dogs.

She is dead tired and falls asleep with her shoes on, her face red from the sun. Chan helps her remove her shoes. At home, they have been sleeping in separate rooms for years after Thomas moved out. There is a small bed in the study, and he sleeps there. There was never any discussion about the matter. It just occurred, like how a path might develop across a field over time. It all seemed natural.

She sleeps in the master bedroom, and he moved his clothes over gradually as well as his books. Military history and tropical birds. He set up a computer and learnt to use it and exchanged e-mails with his circle of friends. She never tries to understand the concept of the internet. They eat together, occasionally going to the coffee shop and sharing a plate of rice because both their appetites have shrunk. She always finishes the vegetables even if they are overcooked to tastelessness.

The thought of lying next to her seems strange. He pulls some sheets from the drawer and sleeps on the rattan sofa although his back hurts. At times, he looks over to the bed and her feet, which face him, and thinks of going over to comfort her. But the thought of the intimacy is unenticing. It might bring about momentary joy, like tasting a long forgotten sweet, but he would probably want to spit right after. Eventually, tiredness wins out, and he wakes with the sun on his face. His wife is looking right at him and asking him where her shoes are.

Chan goes out to find some breakfast. It is another day. Kids in thin shirts are cannonballing into the swimming pool. Flower petals are strewn around the corridors. The smell of spicy food and basil fills his nostrils. He can hear the chatter of the staff. The city is shedding its tragedy already, which leaves a bad taste in his mouth.

He remembers the morgue with all the bodies on the floor waiting to be identified. He cannot venture the thought of returning there. Maybe he could ask for photographs to be shown; it would be easier.

He feels the lure of home. He rarely travels. The last time was to Penang for golf with friends. His wife, on the other hand, goes away three to four times a year, usually with colleagues. She even joins group tours on her own but never asks if he likes to come along.

A shuttlecock is fluttering over the wall, and birds stare at the invader of their space with disinterest. Chan does not go back to the room but continues on. It is three blocks to the sea. He can hear the waves.

The sea is calm. It is not raging. The water is lapping. There are pieces of wood floating about, but it is serene. It smells of suntan oil. If it had a temper, it is now still.

There is a tap on his shoulder.

"Sir, you Singaporean?" He turns and sees a woman, not unattractive, with a worried look on her face. Her belly button is exposed.

"Yes," he said.

"Good. Sometimes hard to tell. Last time Chinaman come here, dress badly, but now they dress better. Sometimes same as Singaporean."

"You want spend time together?" she asks.

"I'm not here for that," he says.

"Sorry sir. You lost someone?"

"I'm trying to find my son," he says. No, he is not lost.

"I see. Sorry sir, business slow. Everyone sad. Heavy heart."

Chan turns to face her. She is more attractive than he thought, even with a plain face without makeup. She is young, with a faded frangipani in her hair and red lips.

"My friend. Gone. Cannot find. I pray for her. But maybe she happier in new life. Husband beat every night. She cry until morning. Tears turn eyes red."

He wonders why she tells him that story.

He reaches into his wallet and extracts some baht and hands it to her. She takes it and makes a small bow, and he walks off back to the hotel.

They go to the centre again and stick up posters on the way. They are untranslated. They watch the news; there has been no new appearance or rescue. Only the dead being retrieved from fallen buildings and roads.

They find out from the airline that their son did arrive a day before the tsunami. They are still trying to track down the hotel where he might be staying. It is a small link and confirms their fears. His wife now stares at the counters, waiting for news. There are still about forty to fifty people here. The decorations are faded, and the fans, mounted on pillars, create a wrecking noise, seemingly ready to tear themselves away.

Chan wanders out. He buys cigarettes and smokes them, a habit he has not imbibed for almost twenty years. The smoke helps him to forget the incense that fills the streets and fills him with calm.

He buys some cakes and biscuits and goes back to the crisis centre to wait. Everyone wears a grim face. A reporter tries to stop him, but he does not want to comment. What does he care to say? An actualisation of hope is much, but all he wants now is the answer to a simple question: is his son alive or dead? It is he who wants answers.

His wife is still staring at the counter. She says that someone from the Singapore High Commission came to talk to her. A young girl in her mid-twenties who wore a black jacket even though the room was hot and stuffy. She took down her name and said that her people would do all they could to find Thomas. The girl's name was Lillian, and she held her hand and gave her a card with a phone number.

"Maybe you should call her," she said.

"Now? If there was any new information, she would have told us. You gave her my number?"

"I did. You've been smoking," she said.

Chan nods. There are other people smoking in the centre. It is the only way to survive the heat and the fear.

"It's not good for you. My colleague, his lungs turned black," she says.

"It's just one cigarette. Maybe one pack at most," he says.

Lillian is with them the whole day, and the conversation has exhausted. She responds whenever she is asked, but Mrs. Chan does not wish to seek solace in her. Chan whispers to Mrs. Chan to let her go, and Mrs. Chan informs Lillian that there is no need to stay around. They know that she knows as much as they know.

Lillian bows and thanks them and hopes that Thomas will be found soon. She takes the flyers and says that she will paste them up around the High Commission.

There is sand on the ground. Mr. Chan goes out for another smoke. His wife does not need him there; she has never needed him there. There is another woman smoking here. She looks like she is in her mid-twenties. She is dressed in a sarong and also having a cigarette. The fingers clasping it are long and thin.

She finishes one and tries to smoke another. Chan counts the motorcycles going past. He is up to five when she asks him if he has a lighter. He takes the newly bought clear green lighter and lights her cigarette. He is surprised how steady his hands are. She thanks him and mentions that her name is Selene.
"Why are you here?" Selene said.
"Our son was here during the tsunami."
Selene looks like she wishes she had not opened her mouth.
"My boyfriend was here too. I had a headache, so stayed in the room. I didn't know what happened until I saw the floor was full of water."
"Have they found him?"
"There is no sign of him. And the night before, we had an argument over my headache."
"What are you going to do now?"
"I don't think I can wait much longer. I have to go back to work," she said.
There is not much sorrow in her eyes. Chan knows that the loss is not great enough to paralyse her. She will be past this mourning soon.
"You should," he says. "If he is gone, what can be done?"
She takes his words in and blows out a great cloud of smoke. Her eyes start to tear. They do not speak as he continues to count the bikes. He notices the still bright blue polish on her fingernails. He counts up to seven before she leaves and disappears, and he never sees her again.
That night, he wakes up from his time on the couch and hears a whispering sound. He looks to the bed, and his wife is not there. He carefully steps over to the bathroom and waits outside. He hears her talking. She seems to be on the phone. He presses his ear to the door. She is on the phone and calling his name. He hears her sobs and goes back to the couch but does not sleep. When he sees her emerge and plop on the bed, he goes to check

the phone once she has fallen asleep. He sees the recent calls and realises that there are more than thirty calls to his son's phone. She has been leaving messages, trying to call him back from the sea.

They are at the crisis centre. The number of people have dwindled over the past few days. Some have found their relatives; others made their peace. It is becoming quieter. Lillian, the girl from the Consul, has gone back to Bangkok but has left her number and promised to call if she hears any news.

A Thai man comes in, wearing a grey shirt. He scans the people in the centre. He is holding a flyer. Chan sits up and notices that it is their flyer. Chan raises one of his spare flyers. The man spots them and marches over. Chan takes out a mint and pops it into his mouth. He has been smoking almost a pack a day since he started.

"You want to see your son?" the man says. His skin is chocolate dark. His teeth jutted out of his mouth, and a tattoo of a mermaid lay over his lower chest.

"Yes. Where is he?"

"Come with me," the man said. "Call me Tai."

"I don't have much money."

"I don't want money. Just come with me. Bring your wife."

Mr Chan follows.

"Here," the man says, pointing to a room.

Is it a scam? Will they be robbed once they step in? But the man has not asked them to bring money. The Chans walk through the door and find themselves in a dark room. Black cloth covers the windows.

There are monitors pushed against the wall. There is a man sitting in front of them, and stacked on a table are an army of digital video cameras. Next to them lies a stack of wanted posters, some clumsily torn.

"Sit," he says.

"We have been watching tapes from the cameras. We were doing a documentary to promote this hotel. After disaster, nobody want. We went to look at tapes. And then we see all these people, and then one of them is on these posters.

"Then Chai, my friend, have idea. We watch videos, find faces."

Chan shakes. This is not what he has expected. He is raging with anger. But Mrs. Chan is more agreeable.

"You find my son? You see him?"

"Yes," says Tai. He speaks to his friend in Thai, and Chai takes out a tape. There is a sheet of paper with a list of codes.

"In two tapes. We find your son," he says.

The big man places the tape delicately into the camera and lets it close. He starts rewinding the tape, and a barrage of images fly past. Mrs. Chan has to close her eyes.

The tape stops rewinding, and it starts playing.

"In the back. In the back," Tai says, pointing to one of the monitors.

The Chans stare at the screen. Mrs. Chan steadies herself and sits down on one of the chairs. There is a smiling Caucasian woman on the screen. Mrs. Chan wonders if she might be a victim as well. She is describing the beauty of the beach and how perfect the sunlight is.

"There! There!" he shouts.

They see Thomas walk across in the background. He has a can of Coke in his hand. There is a woman with him, and neither of them recognises who she is. He finishes the can of Coke. The woman has started to talk about the excellent food they had and the party she was at, and Thomas throws away the can and walks off.

"That is him? Do you want me to rewind?"

Mr. Chan nods. The tape is rewound and played again. And

again. They watch it three times.

"Is he saying something? Can we hear?"

"Too far sir. The cameras cannot pick up voice from so far," Tai says.

"We put in other tape now?" Tai continues.

Mrs. Chan nods. The editor digs through the tapes and takes one out and sticks it in.

The tape is rewound, and now Mrs. Chan cannot take her eyes off the screen.

"Here," Tai says.

It is a tape of their son. He is dancing. The same woman is with him. He wears sunglasses and is bare-chested, with big orange Bermudas. Their son is wearing a necklace, and part of his skin looks burnt and red. They are at a party of some sort.

The camera turns to him.

"Are you having fun?" the narrator says.

"Yes!" Thomas replies. It is his voice. Mrs. Chan presses her hand onto the monitor. The big man protests, but Tai says something, and he shuts up.

"What are you here for?" The narrator continues.

"Some diving. Good food. Get away from work," he says.

"All right." And the camera turns to his companion.

"And you?" The companion shakes her head. She does not want to be interviewed. The cameraman then enters the hotel to interview other people.

"Again," Mr. Chan says. Mrs. Chan stays on the monitor.

They play the tape three more times. Then Tai gets a bit annoyed.

"There are other people. We can make copy for you."

"Son . . . nowhere else?"

"I don't see," Tai says.

Mr. Chan drags his wife away from the screen, and they leave. The sun has emerged and is pouring onto the world.

"I'm staying here," said Mrs. Chan.

"I will help them look over the tapes."

"You don't know any Thai. We are almost out of money," he said.

"Transfer some money over. I have savings. I will remain here."

"He's gone," Mr. Chan says.

"I don't know that. His body is not found."

Because it is probably eaten by fishes and turtles. Mr. Chan shudders to think about it.

"I am going back."

"Then go," she says. "I can change my flight."

"I will send money over," he says.

She nods. "I am going to the beach."

"Call me every day," he says.

But this is the point of breaking, where their bound fate cracks, and they know the future has formed where they no longer are together.

On the flight back, he does not dare to stare out into the sea. Only when they are landing in Singapore, the world a dull grey, does he dare to look out the window onto the towers of the gleaming city. The lights are coming on all at the same time as the plane comes in, and the city is lit by tiny lights, ready for the engulfing night.

When he goes back to the flat, he notes the emptiness. He calls the hotel where she is, but she is not in the room. He decides not to leave a message for her. He then takes a taxi to his son's apartment. He knocks on the door, and someone is in. A bald Indian man with bulging biceps named Ravi. He tells Mr. Chan that he is Thomas's housemate. Chan tells him what has happened, and he is in shock.

"He was such a nice boy," Ravi says. Ravi works for a merchant bank and spends half his time out of Singapore, which suited Thomas just fine.

"I'm sorry, but will there be a wake?"

Mr. Chan has not even thought about it. Will there be one? Without a body? With his wife not yet giving him up?

He starts to pack things up, and Ravi helps. Ravi asks if he can keep the CD player because they paid for it together, and Mr. Chan says yes. He tells Ravi to take whatever he wants, but he only takes a few CDs and books.

Chan finds a photograph of Thomas and the woman in the videos. It is placed above the headboard. Chan asks Ravi, and Ravi says she came over sometimes.

Ravi nods. "I'm sorry, but I never spoke to her. Just saw her shoes in the morning."

Chan pauses and starts packing, holding every item as if he were an archaeologist unearthing remains of a burial site.

It is four in the morning when he has everything put away. Ravi has gone to sleep at one as he has an early meeting. There are about ten boxes. He will need a pickup truck to get them all. Ravi had muttered something about the rent. They will need to talk to the landlord. Maybe he could get back a deposit, but Chan has no energy for these things.

He falls asleep on the boxes and is shaken awake by Ravi, who is dressed in a suit.

"Sir, I must go. You take care. I leave the extra key with you," he says.

Chan can only wave weakly. Ravi goes out of the door, and Chan sees the sandals and shoes arrayed next to the door.

So many things to keep. What would be the point? Perhaps he could give them away or let Ravi do it.

Chan lets himself out and takes a taxi home. The driver is so quiet that he falls asleep. When he reaches home, he takes out the photographs that Thomas had. He goes to make a cup of coffee for himself.

Then he heads to the bank and does a money transfer to his wife. A bank staff helps him along and instructs him. She calls him to tell him that she will check and hangs up.

She calls him three days later, while he is having chicken rice wrapped in grease paper, to tell him that she has received the money.

"We found him in more tapes," she says. "Two more."

"What was he doing?" he says.

"He was walking away in one. I can tell from his back. In the other, he is getting into a pedicab."

"All very short?"

"About twenty seconds. Do you want me to send the footage? They can make copies?"

"No. Not for that."

He imagines her palm pressed to the screen whenever he appears.

"Any more progress in the search?"

"They are still looking."

"I have packed up his things."

"Oh," she says. He can see the image of her in his mind.

"Let me know if you hear anything and when you want to come back."

"Chan?" she says over the phone.

"Yes?" "Can you check . . . if there are old phone messages from him? Can you keep them?"

He agrees. All he wants now is to be rid of her voice; the distance is now clearly more than physical. She has gravitated away to a point in the world he can no longer understand.

They hang up, and he goes back to his meal and the television. Snow starts to appear on the screen, but he continues to watch even though the noise makes the dialogue incomprehensible.

Chan takes out the last of the cigarettes and smokes them as the television scatters random noise and light into the living room.

When Chan calls his wife, she says that she has moved to an apartment next to the crisis centre. He carefully tells her what has been going on at his side, and the line seems to be constantly cut with static as if the spirits do not want her to hear.

"You should come back," he says.

"I will when I know," she says, hanging up. Chan listens to the light sound of the phone for a while before putting away the receiver. He sees the boxes around him and takes out a CD. It says Ella Fitzgerald. He puts it inside the DVD player and lets it play, and the soothing voice of a woman he has never heard before wafts through the room. He never knew anyone could sing like that, and he lets the CD play over and over until the night arrives.

It is Thomas's fourteenth birthday. They are at Swensen's for the occasion. It was his decision to come here after Mrs. Chan asked him how he wanted to celebrate. At first, Chan wanted to tell him to bring his friends, but he felt awkward about it. They are at the airport, and they have a seat near the window. They stare out of the window at the passing planes, and the roar of the aircraft occasionally makes their spoons and table shiver.

It is the moment of his great departure, the last moment where he might view his parents as being part of his circle. Chan cannot remember ever going out for ice cream. Buying Cornettos from the ice cream man or the neighbourhood shop, certainly, but never actually going to an ice cream parlour and sitting down like at a restaurant. Thomas orders eagerly and asks for water for his parents.

The universes they are in are splitting, and this is the last time he even considers celebrating his birthday with them. The ice cream comes, and there is a small cake with a candle on it. Mrs. Chan sings a soft Happy Birthday song, hardly discernible above the muzak. Chan knows that his wife finds the ice cream too sweet, but she keeps her comments to herself and smiles for her son.

Should they order real food? Chan asks, but his son warns that the food isn't any good here.

"People only come here for the ice cream, Pa," he says, a smile on his face.

As he is about to blow out the candle, Thomas reaches out his arms, and Chan and his wife each take his hand. A plane is passing overhead, and the table is shivering very slightly. Thomas says that he is so happy that they are there as Chan realises how cold his fingers are.

Understudies

Jeffrey Lim

Feeling tied down? Want to get out now? Change your skin? Like to be someone else? Fill in this form in duplicate, and submit it to the Human Resources manager.

Beta Sydney studied the form carefully.

Name of principal

He pressed the mechanical pencil to the paper and scrawled: "Wong Sydney"

Name of understudy

He sniffed. "Beta Sydney, surname Wong."

Period spent understudying

He counted off his fingers. "Twelve years."

Desired new principal

Without hesitation, Beta Sydney wrote: "Anyone else."

Reasons for application

Here, Beta Sydney had to think.

Sydney was a model citizen.

He had been streamed into the best classes. He spent four sterling years in Raffles Institution where he was a prefect and champion rugby captain. In Raffles Junior College, he was President of the student council. His A-level exams results were all As and distinctions.

During National Service, he was the recipient of an Officer

Cadet School sword of honour. They gave him a scholarship to Harvard. He dutifully accepted.

He married into money—a rich Chinese wife, and a doctor to boot. They had four children when the government publicly encouraged babies.

Map out every route one can take for the perfect Singaporean life, and chances were that you would be tracing Sydney Wong's footsteps.

At one point, the very perfection of his record was considered a threat. The Monitors who watched him discreetly were anxious that they would have no means by which they could seize control of his life and blackmail him into submission.

And then, just as they were about to consider him a threat, a foible materialised. He appeared to have a predilection for speeding. A speed camera caught him ripping by at 90 km per hour in a 60 km-per-hour speed zone more than three times.

They were satisfied. It was a harmless vice, but a vice nonetheless.

No one dreamed of calling in his understudy.

•

His mother, Hui Ling, used to tell him that she knew the very morning he had arrived as she stood on the verandah of their family home.

"I let your father sleep," she said. "And when the sun came up, I knew you were here." She would reach down to her belly, press her hand against it, and move it in a slow, languid circle.

"Here, in me."

Sydney could still remember her long dark hair as it brushed against his face when he was still small enough to be carried in her arms. He remembered how she smelt of milk and cereal. He remembered how she was able to turn every latest tune into a lullaby as she hummed him to sleep, the melodies drifting around him like her scent, as he succumbed to the afternoon heat.

His father, Kim Soon, disliked the attention she gave him. "He's going to grow up to be a mommy's boy," he complained.

Sydney's abiding memory of his father was of him sitting at the dining table hunched over a newspaper or a magazine. He found it difficult to remember if his father ever looked up from his reading.

Hui Ling moved over into the living room and sat down by her son, "I think he's going to be a sculptor."

His father sniffed contemptuously and turned a page. "Engineer, doctor, lawyer, accountant . . . all these you don't want," Kim Soon threw his eyes over the obituaries, and sniffed contemptuously. "Sculp-tor."

In school, he showed a facility for art. In his spare time, he joined an arts and crafts group at his local Community Centre. Once he sat himself down before a canvas with paints, his hands would move over it at an almost magical speed and, gradually, works emerged which amazed his seniors.

And then, one night, when he was eight, as he was trying to sleep, he overheard his parents arguing, their voices coming through the bedroom wall.

"Why does he have to take these classes?" His mother seemed agitated.

"We're supposed to . . . Will you stop being so stubborn?" His father sounded exasperated.

"I want to raise my son my own way. He's good at arts, and I want him to go to an arts school," she said.

"What," his father seemed angry, "do you think you can just do what you want? Right now, the government says that art is a waste of time. Don't you know that they're sending all the useless boys to study those classes?"

"I don't care," she said, "he's happiest when he's doing his art.

He's got talent."

A short pause followed after which he heard his father say:

"You know they will replace you if you keep improvising like this."

•

Please provide details of proposed new principal.

Beta Sydney scratched his chin and wrote.

"Don't know, don't care. Make me a road sweeper. Trash collector. *Anybody* else." He paused, then wrote:

"Really am open to new ideas. No joking."

Sydney returned home to see his four children hard at work. The youngest, little Joel, was reading his picture book, precocious for a three-year-old. His wife, Melanie, was still at the hospital. The maid, Imelda, was making dinner, and the living room was filled with the aroma of her cooking.

He walked out to the porch of his bungalow and stretched. As he had learnt to do, he watched the street without appearing to watch, surveyed the houses around him without giving any indication that he was surveying anything.

Were the Monitors there, watching?

•

He remembered the very last afternoon his mother was with him. She had taken him to see a dentist, and she had gone outside to wait when the dentist finished the last of the cleaning up.

"The mother has not been performing," the dentist said. The light mounted onto the strap around his forehead blinded Sydney's eyes every time he looked up into them, so he closed his eyes.

"Mmm... so dangerous," the nurse nodded. The nurse moved the plastic suction pipe to the other side of Sydney's tongue. He could hear a loud sucking sound as it cleared saliva.

"Well," Dr. Tan said calmly as he angled the mirror to Sydney's upper jaw, "if you don't do what they tell you to, it's your own fault."

"What about the boy?" the nurse asked.

Sydney wasn't sure, but he could swear that she was referring to him.

"So far so good," Dr. Tan replied. "Let's hope he's like his father."

Later, the nurse led Sydney out of the room to his mother who had been reading a magazine. The waiting room was small, with a few leather seats by the sides of the walls and a glass wall overlooking Thomson Road. Sydney could see the red SBS Mercedes buses with their round headlights and the blue construction lorries caked in orange mud passing by. Dr. Tan's English and Chinese names were printed in reverse on the glass.

"Twenty dollars," the nurse announced.

Hui Ling reached into her purse and pulled out her wallet.

"So, when are you going to have another child?"

The nurse asked as she offered Hui Ling change.

Hui Ling hardly paused before answering. "Oh no, one is enough."

Sydney heard the silence that followed. He turned his head slowly back to look at them. Dr. Tan and the nurse seemed to be genuinely at a loss for words as Hui Ling handed the notes over.

"Two," the nurse said nervously as she took the money.

"Sorry?" Hui Ling asked.

"It's 'two is enough'," the nurse corrected her.

"Nonsense," Hui Ling replied with a wave of her hand, "my hands are full as it is."

Another audible silence followed.

The telephone rang. Sydney noticed that everyone in the room seemed to jump when it broke the silence.

The nurse took a deep breath and visibly composed herself. She lifted the receiver to her ear. "Tan Clinic."

There was a little pause as the nurse listened. Sydney noticed his mother gripping her wallet tightly.

The nurse handed the phone over to Hui Ling.

"It's for you."

Hui Ling took the receiver with the air of a person who was about to speak with someone very unpleasant. "Hello?"

His mother's eyes darted nervously about her and then they rested on him. Sydney felt a cold sensation go down his back, leaving goose bumps in its wake.

"Yes, yes, I understand . . . Goodbye," she said quietly.

She handed the receiver back to the nurse who took it without comment. She leaned against the counter and gripped its edge to steady herself. Her shoulders rose as she drew a deep breath, and her body shook as she expelled it.

The nurse tapped her shoulder and gestured to Sydney, as if to remind her that her son was watching.

Hui Ling stepped back from the counter and turned to Sydney. She took him resolutely by the hand and made for the door.

"Let's go home," she said.

The car ride back was unusually quiet. Sydney found himself watching her, waiting for her to say something.

When they came home, Hui Ling put a piece of chocolate cake she bought from a Polar Café in Thomson Plaza and placed the slice on a blue dinner plate. She filled a small plastic glass with milky pink *bandung*.

"I have to go out for a while," she said as she placed the food on the living room table next to his toys. Her hands were trembling and she kept rubbing her eyes and sniffing.

"Where are you going?" Sydney asked.

Hui Ling held a hand to her mouth and took a deep breath through her nose. Her eyes were glistening and her face was red. She knelt by his side. "Be a good boy and wait for me to come back. Okay? ... Mommy loves you very much."

He remembered her stepping back to look at him as if trying her best to memorise every little detail about him.

A moment later, she was out the door.

He sat through an afternoon matinee. The men in the movie wore bell-bottom pants and shirts that had swirling psychedelic patterns with high collars. To him, they looked unhappy even though their eyes were hidden behind square sunglasses or under moppish haircuts.

After the movie had finished, he heard the door latch open and the jingling of his mother's keys. He ran to the door to greet her.

But as he came up to her, he noticed that she was no longer wearing her floral dress and that she had trimmed her hair. She smelt different too. The aroma of nail polish soured in his mouth as he approached her.

"Mommy?" he asked. "Where have you been?"

She looked at him with a strange detachment.

"Just out, darling. Just out."

•

Beta Sydney straightened his shirt and smoothed back his hair. The interview was not going well.

"We sympathise," the Lead HR Manager replied, "unfortunately, there's only so much we can do."

Beta Sydney felt uncomfortable. It was a large room, with a long table at one end where the four HR Managers were seated.

The Lead HR Manager continued. "The application forms are not meant for Grade One personalities like your principal's. Too much resources have already been invested in training you to let you swap."

"Can't you get a replacement?" Beta Sydney replied.

A second HR Manager, a plump woman with a pinched face, snapped. "Do you think we can entertain just any request for a change just like that? If we let your application through, then every single Grade One understudy will also fill in these forms." Here, she lifted the form he had filled in, waving it as though it was a piece of toilet paper.

"You should have read the line at the bottom of the form: 'Not Applicable for Grade One understudies'," she said resolutely.

"Be patient," the Lead HR Manager replied. "Your principal will eventually stop being Grade One, and you can apply then."

It was Beta Sydney's turn to chafe. "That could take forever!"

"No," a third HR Manager, a thin Indian man replied, "If he changes his job and stops doing the work we've assigned him, we will take him off the Grade One list."

"Or," the fourth HR Manager, a dark Malay man with sunglasses, chimed in, "maybe he will make a mistake . . . Do something that will force us to swap you."

Beta Sydney shook his head. "He doesn't make mistakes. He's a bloody boy scout. I should've known better than to hope you would listen."

He got up and slammed the door behind him as he left.

In the room, the plump woman leaned over to the Lead HR Manager, "Why don't we just give in to his request?"

The Lead HR Manager shook his head. "If we have no approval, we cannot do anything."

Sydney was certain the Monitors were not looking or listening. He tapped his fingers on the table, chewing his lip as the phone rang.

"Hello," the voice answered on the line.
"You know who I am?"
There was a long pause.
"Are you being monitored?"
"Not right now," Sydney answered, keeping his voice low.
There was a shorter pause.
"Well, what do you want?"
Sydney spoke quickly, "I have a proposal for you."

•

Sydney's best friend, Soon Cheng, was a "difficult" student. He was always being "called up" by the principal, making a formal apology to someone during assembly or being made to stand up by their irate teachers in class.

Mr. Ho appeared to hate Soon Cheng the most. Their balding math teacher had buck-teeth, a diminutive chin and heavy dark- rimmed glasses that he occasionally pushed back over the ridge of a short nose. His fingers were always white with chalkboard powder, and he habitually smeared them against the slacks he wore, which were always either grey or brown.

One day, Mr. Ho was returning test sheets to the class, a ritual that involved having their names and test scores read out loudly as they each went to the front of the class to collect their papers. Mr. Ho flipped through the sheets, licking his fingers as he did so, until he stopped at one test sheet.

"Tay Soon Cheng," Mr. Ho said, lifting one out of the pile. "18 out of 100."

Soon Cheng dragged himself to his feet and made his way to the front of the class, his face a mask of displeasure.

Before the boy came within a few desks of the front, Mr. Ho took his test sheet and crumpled it. Soon Cheng stopped in his tracks. The noisy crackling of the paper was the only sound audible for a long while. Mr. Ho tossed the round ball of mangled paper, hitting Soon Cheng in the face.

They all heard what Mr. Ho said next, "Go back home to your father's noodle stall and stop wasting my time!"

Mr. Ho returned to the other papers and continued as though nothing had happened. "Melvin Low, 62 out of 100."

Quietly, Soon Cheng bent down, picked up the test paper, biting his lower lip as he did so. Sydney was convinced the boy was going to pounce on his teacher. His classmates were too. Melvin Low skirted nervously around him to retrieve his paper from Mr. Ho, avoiding him the way one would a dangerous animal.

Later that day, Sydney and Soon Cheng were on the school basketball court, playing a one-on-one game.

Basketball was the only thing Soon Cheng excelled at. Though their team was regularly defeated by schools like Chung Cheng or River Valley and was one of the few failures in a school full of winners, Sydney and Soon Cheng found it comforting to be on a losing team. It helped to keep expectations low.

"Enough," Sydney came to a halt, panting heavily, gripping his shorts and bending over.

Soon Cheng, who wasn't tired, dribbled the ball out to the three-point line and began lofting his jumpers through the net, calmly swishing the shots in without touching the rim.

"Don't listen to Mr. Ho," Sydney ventured. He had been waiting to say this since class ended.

"I hate this school," Soon Cheng replied. His next shot rimmed out again to a litany of curses. His hands dropped to his sides and settled on his hips.

Sydney collected the rebound.

"Why don't you study with me?"

Soon Cheng looked irritated. "What?"

"Let's study for the common test."

Soon Cheng shook his head. "No lah, I don't have time. I have to go back to help at my father's stall."

"Okay, then every day after school, instead of basketball, we study."

Soon Cheng regarded his friend for moment. "Why? You want to be my tuition teacher ah? I got no money you know."

"I'll settle for noodles," Sydney replied, challenging him.

Soon Cheng stopped and looked at him.

"Pass me the ball," he said softly.

•

"What you're proposing," Michael said, stirring his tea vigorously, "is incredibly risky."

"Isn't the money good enough?" Sydney asked, leaning back into his chair. His eyes surveyed the crowd passing by the Starbucks at Raffles City. Expertly, he satisfied himself that there were no Monitors present.

"We can do this," Michael replied. "But are you sure your children and wife will come?"

Sydney nodded. "Yes. We're not happy."

Michael shook his head. "That's not good enough. Have you *asked* them?"

Sydney managed a straight stare without blinking. "Of course."

"And they're okay with it?"

Sydney nodded.

He hadn't asked Melanie. Still, it wasn't hard to know what she was thinking. If Michael needed confirmation, he would talk to her that night. For now, Sydney reasoned, it was better to settle everything now.

"We'll set up everything in three months," Michael continued. He flipped through a file on his lap. "Buenos Aires, you say?"

Sydney nodded. "Far away from here."

"Our fees must be paid upfront. After that, we will contact you to confirm payment and finalise some details," Michael said. He gulped some tea. "About two months from now, you'll need to make sure that all funds are transferred to your new accounts ... We'll also confirm the new addresses and passports."

"How will you get these to me?" Sydney asked.

"Don't worry," Michael replied. "You just worry about making sure everything else is ready."

All through the years, Sydney had been careful, behaving himself as best as he could. An immaculate record was hard to maintain but he knew it was necessary.

It hadn't been easy, but doing everything that was expected of him was the only way to make sure he could fly under their radar and make ready his escape.

He was even smart enough to get a few speeding tickets in case his record got too clean for their comfort.

It was just a matter of planning.

They were not supposed to visit their principals. It was a severe breach of the rules. Still, Beta Sydney felt he had to do it. The taxi left him on the street outside the bungalow. The lights were on at home in the children's room and the master bedroom.

They must be home, he thought.

Not for the first time, he toyed with the idea of knocking on their door and introducing himself.

Why not? How often does one shake up their world completely, he thought.

"Hello, Mr. Wong!"

Beta Sydney's heart jumped. Someone had seen him. He turned. It was a neighbour.

"Oh, hello," Beta Sydney recovered quickly, slipping into his role. It felt odd to play out the role now, as if it were some impromptu rehearsal.

"Out for a late night stroll?" The neighbour was an old Eurasian man. Mr. Rodrigues, Beta recalled.

"Oh yes," Beta Sydney said, relaxing a little. *If HR knew what he was doing now, they'd have his skin*, he thought. Somehow, that thought seemed comforting. "Good weather tonight, so just taking a short walk."

"And Mrs. Wong?" Beta Sydney assumed she was in the bedroom. "Oh," he said, "she's busy."

Mr. Rodrigues nodded. "Doctors . . . they work so hard."

Beta Sydney shrugged. "Yes, they do."

It was Mr. Rodrigues who broke the uncomfortable pause. "Okay, see you later."

Beta Sydney smiled and waved the old gentleman off. He breathed a sigh of relief when he was gone.

What was he thinking, standing out here? Just what did he want to do?

Beta Sydney shook his head and made his way discreetly into the shadows.

●

Sydney learnt what happened when you didn't follow their script when Soon Cheng disappeared in Secondary Three.

They had been working together on their math. Eventually, there came a day when Mr. Ho was standing in class returning test scripts to the students.

"Tay Soon Cheng," Mr. Ho intoned, lifting the results of their common test out from the pile. Soon Cheng rose but was unable to take another step from his desk to collect his paper. The other classmates were urging him forward in muted whispers.

"Go! Go! ... Why you never go ..."

"Oi, teacher calling you, lah ..."

"Hurry up, hurry up ..."

Mr. Ho lifted his glasses off his nose and brought the sheet within an inch of his eyes, squinting at the results. A short moment later, a scowl broke out over his features. Soon Cheng sagged visibly.

"Tay Soon Cheng," he repeated.

"Go ... Come on, hurry up ..."

"Don't make him angry ..."

"83 out of 100." Mr. Ho stuck out his hand with the test sheet clasped firmly. The whispers came to a halt. Soon Cheng took a moment for the result to register.

Mr. Ho's other hand was already pulling another sheet out. "Ang Cheng Hock," he continued, "66 out of 100."

Soon Cheng's shot clanged off the rim. He bounded across the court to collect the rebound and grabbed it just over Sydney's outstretched hands.

"Wah, if I study anymore with you, I'm going to lose all my basketball kungfu." Soon Cheng laughed as he came away with the ball.

"As if," Sydney said, gasping for air and gripping his knees. Soon Cheng had hardly broken a sweat. "Eh, this game is a one-off treat before we start studying for the O-levels."

"Okay, okay lah!" Soon Cheng threw up another shot and laughed. It missed horribly. Sydney left the rebound alone and nursed his aching lungs.

"My father will be happy," Soon Cheng said suddenly, still looking at the basketball rim. He chuckled. "He will probably think I cheated."

Sydney dropped to the ground, threw his hands behind him to prop himself up and stuck his legs out, still catching his breath.

Soon Cheng regarded him with slanted eyes. "Eh," he said.

"What?" Sydney asked.

"Thank you."

Sydney stared at him for a while and then shook his head, taking a deep breath. "So how? You owe me dinner. Noodles also can," he said, wiping sweat from his brow.

"Tay Soon Cheng!"

It was Mr. Ho's voice.

He was standing by the court and gesturing to Soon Cheng with his hands.

"Come, boy, I want to talk to you."

Sydney watched as his friend made his way to the teacher. He followed them with his eyes as they went around the corner into a shaded part of the adjacent school canteen.

He lay back against the court, feeling the heat soaking through his drenched T-shirt and smelling the salty tang of his sweat. In the pale blue sky above him, Sydney tracked a slow moving cloud, watching the slipstreams around the edges unravelling in slow motion. Soon Cheng did not return until it had passed fully out of his sight.

"What took you so long?" Sydney asked.

Soon Cheng was walking slowly now, as if measuring his steps, plodding his way back to the court. He calmly made his way to his belongings. There was something different about him.

Sydney tried again. "Oi, what's the matter? I'm talking to you."

Soon Cheng shook his head, "Sorry, I'm going home." He seemed subdued, almost apologetic.

"What? Why?" Sydney asked.

"My father needs me," Soon Cheng said strapping on his digital watch and slinging his bag over his shoulder.

"Are you okay?" Sydney asked.

"See you tomorrow," Soon Cheng said as he turned and made

his way briskly off the court.

Soon Cheng never stayed to work with Sydney on his studies again. He wore a mask of irritation every time Sydney broached the subject of after-school work and soon Sydney stopped asking. Gradually, Soon Cheng took to spending more time at his father's noodle stall.

By the time the O-level results came out, there was no surprise waiting for Soon Cheng. When he came back to school to collect his results, Sydney noticed that he had let his hair grow long, sported an earring, and had a pager strapped to his belt. He held a lit cigarette in one hand.

Soon Cheng sauntered into the school hall, queued and took his results slip. Sydney called out to him. Soon Cheng saw him coming and quickly folded the paper, stuffing it into his pocket.

"How?" Sydney asked.

Soon Cheng shrugged. "So-so," he replied, putting the cigarette to his mouth and drawing a deep breath, his eyes looking elsewhere.

•

Melanie refused.

"I can't leave all this," she said, her eyes watering. "Why would I want to go?"

"Haven't you been listening?" Sydney asked. "We're all being watched. If you put one step out of line, they'll change you. Swap you with some replacement."

Melanie shook her head. "You're scaring me," she said. "You sound like you're having a breakdown again."

This mystified Sydney.

"What did you say?"

"I said you sound like you're having a breakdown again."

Sydney shook his head. "What are you talking about? I've

never had a breakdown before."

It was then that he realised that Melanie seemed different.

"Oh my God," he said. "They found out, didn't they? . . . Y-You're a *replacement*."

He pointed at her, his hand shaking. Melanie seemed disgusted but quickly regained her composure. She shook her head.

"Oh Sydney," she put her hand to her mouth to suppress what seemed to him to be an exaggerated gasp of horror. "I thought the doctor had cured you."

"When?" Sydney demanded. "When did you replace her? . . . Where is she? Where's my Melanie?"

Beta Sydney awoke with a start. His handphone was buzzing, rattling against the surface of his bedside table.

He reached out and picked it up, putting it to his ear.

"Hello?"

The voice on the other side was emotionless and direct.

"Standby. Principal replacement underway."

He sat up, still clutching the phone.

"Say again?" he asked, eyes widening.

The voice remained colourlessly impassive.

"Principal replacement underway."

Sydney took Rebecca by her shoulders and turned her round to face him. Her hands were raised defensively and she was recoiling. His other daughter, Julie, was squatting in the corner of the bathroom, hugging herself.

"Daddy," Rebecca said angrily, "Let-me-go!"

"What did you say just now? Say it again!" He asked, shaking her.

Rebecca tried to twist free, "You're not following the script!"

He heard Melanie pounding on the door.

"Let me in!" Melanie cried.

"No!" Sydney said, pressing his back against the bathroom door.

"Mommy!" Rebecca was calling out now but warily steering clear of her father's reach.

"What are you doing to them?" Melanie asked. She was pounding on the door now.

"Nothing!" He replied. "I'm not doing anything."

Melanie tried to soften her voice. "Honey," she said, her voice quivering with emotion, "I know this has been a stressful time for you."

"Mommy," Rebecca called. "Make Daddy stop!"

His other daughter, Julie, quietly grabbed at her knees, the fingers pulling at the skin on her kneecaps, her mouth chewing on a lock of hair.

"No one can *make* Daddy do anything," Sydney replied, "Not even Mommy."

"Sydney, stop it!" Melanie called through the door. "If you don't stop this, I'm going to have to call someone."

"Who?" Sydney challenged.

Julie started to cry. Her hands went up and clasped her ears.

"The police. I'll call the police. Now is that what you want?" Melanie yelled.

"You're lying," he said, "I know who you're going to call!"

There was a pause.

"And who am I going to call, Sydney?"

•

Her name was Jessie Rosario.

Whenever Sydney came by to pick her up, her father seemed to watch him from the corner of his eye and always seemed to have something to say without ever quite getting to it.

Sydney raised the topic with Jessie, but she quickly dismissed his fears.

"Don't be paranoid," she said, "My father doesn't have anything against you. He just has difficulty understanding how to let me go."

"Maybe he doesn't like me because I'm not Eurasian," Sydney suggested.

"I've dated other non-Eurasians before, you know," she said.

"And did he dislike them also?"

She rolled her eyes.

"I'm telling you, your father doesn't like me," he muttered.

"So what?" Jessie asked. "Why worry? I am the one who has to like you."

Sydney nodded. "Yes, but it would be nice to have his blessing."

Jessie's mouth dropped open. "His blessing? Why Mr. Sydney Wong..." she said with mock incredulity, "are you thinking what I think you're thinking?"

One day, he sent Jessie home. As the car pulled into Mr. Rosario's driveway, he noticed Mr. Rosario standing on their lawn, a mobile phone pressed against his cheek. In his fifties, Mr. Rosario had greying hair and a sizeable paunch. He paced the lawn with a limp, which Sydney had learnt was the result of some accident he had sustained in his youth. His brow was furrowed as he paced that slow, interrupted gait of his.

Sydney did not like that look.

"Hello Daddy," Jessie said as she came out of the car.

Her father nodded briefly.

They began fishing out their gear from the hatchback and carrying it back into the house. As he walked towards the entrance of the house, Sydney noticed that Mr. Rosario's expression blackened visibly as their eyes met briefly.

"Hello, uncle," Sydney said warily.

Mr. Rosario did not answer.

Later, when Jessie had gone upstairs to change, Mr. Rosario took the chance to pull him over.

"Come with me," Mr. Rosario said flatly. "We need to talk."

They went to the living room. When Sydney had taken his seat, Mr. Rosario's eyes narrowed to a squint.

"My daughter is one of a kind."

"Yes she is," Sydney replied with a friendly, but nervous smile, not sure where this was going.

"No," Mr. Rosario stated forcefully. "I mean, I will not have her replaced."

Sydney found himself blinking rapidly as he struggled to comprehend what he was being told. He found himself scratching his head and looking into Mr. Rosario's eyes. The man stared back, with an unyielding glare.

"Mr. Rosario," he said quickly, "there are many, many mixed couples in Singapore –"

"Sure," Mr. Rosario said, as if seizing on some opportunity that arose in the conversation. "Of course, there are. The ones that are scripted."

Sydney paused for a moment and then shook his head. "I-I don't follow."

"Neither did your mother," Mr. Rosario said, almost contemptuously.

This took Sydney by surprise. Sydney had never mentioned her much to Mr. Rosario. "Why are we talking about her?"

The shrill whistle of Mr. Rosario's mobile telephone interrupted them. He reached into his pocket and took out the telephone, staring at the number on the LCD. His face was a mask of frustration, and his eyes narrowed at the number he saw. The phone rang again. He punched a button and brought the phone to his ear.

"No, I wasn't going to mention it," Mr. Rosario said after a short pause. "Yes, I know the rules. Look, I'm just doing what's best for my family... No, that's not what you said... you said I could take the matter into my hands."

There was another pause, and this one was ended with an unexpected outburst: "Look! If you had done your job and gotten your girl ready by now, I wouldn't be in this position! Have I complained about that? Have I once said anything about that? No! It's your bloody scheduling problems. Well, I don't care!"

As Mr. Rosario's tirade continued, Sydney took the opportunity to excuse himself with a sheepish gesture at his watch and a half-hearted polite wave. He drove home, troubled.

A week later, Sydney's telephone rang and he answered, thinking Jessie was calling to make sure he was leaving on time to pick her up.

"I'm on my way," he insisted as soon as he heard her voice.

"Sydney, listen." Her voice sounded nasal, as if she had a cold. She sounded like she was going to say something very serious. "I've been thinking..."

Sydney quickly surmised that her father had said something.

"Wait, Jessie –"

"It would be best for both of us," she was parcelling out her words, "if we don't see each other any more."

"What? No... Jessie?"

She had hung up, abruptly. When he called her back, he found that the phone had been disconnected.

When he drove down to see her a few days after, he was calmly told by Mrs. Rosario that she did not want any trouble. Jessie, she said, had packed her bags and left for Australia.

No, Mrs. Rosario insisted, this had nothing to do with Jessie's father. No, she insisted, he would not be allowed to find out where Jessie had gone or speak to Mr. Rosario. Mrs. Rosario also suggested politely that he lower his voice and that he leave before she called the police.

Months later, when he was with his friends at Boat Quay,

trying their best to help him relax and forget, one of his friends introduced a young Chinese woman to him. They shook hands. She kept talking to him long after his friends had decided to go home when the pub closed. He took her for a long walk along the Singapore River and listened to her intently, glad to have some company, to take his mind off Jessie.

It was only later that he realised that he had not asked her for her full name.

"It's Melanie Ho," she said. "And what's yours?"

•

"Who do you think am I going to call?" Melanie asked again.

"You know who," he insisted.

"Stop it. You're scaring our children," Melanie said slowly through the door. "And you're scaring me."

Sydney found himself shaking his head, cradling his temple with his palms and struggling to compose himself as he slid down to the floor.

"Mommy, come and get us out of here," Rebecca pleaded.

"Sydney," Melanie pleaded again. "You're just tired and you need help. Now just open the door and let me in and we will take this one step at a time."

"No!"

"Sydney . . ." Melanie's voice dipped. "You shouldn't do this."

"Why not?" That was all Sydney could say now.

"Because they have *understudies*," she replied. "And they won't hesitate to make a change."

Beta Sydney was nervous and happy. The white car with the QX plate pulled up by the kerb. The door opened. He stepped in, happy to be on his way.

As the car sped along towards its destination, he tried to engage the Monitors in conversation. There were two of them in the front seats. Neither looked back to acknowledge his presence.

"So," he said, "what happened?"

"Your principal's been planning an escape for some time," came the reply. The Monitor who was not driving appeared to be the designated communicator with him.

Beta Sydney nodded. "An escape? Really? Wow . . . and I thought he was happy being here . . . How did you discover this?"

"Double agent," came the reply.

Sydney nodded. He had heard of them. Their job was to ferret out anyone trying to cheat the system. HR occasionally referred to them whenever they needed to give a message with a hint of menace.

"Is there anyone else in the house who must be replaced?" Beta Sydney asked. There was a pause so he added, "I need to know, just in case there are any innocents who shouldn't."

"No one. But take note: the children are not supposed to know what is happening," came the reply.

"Okay," Beta Sydney replied, "Got it. So, how are we explaining the switchover? I assume the principal's gone and done something really wrong, how am I supposed to address that?"

The Monitor at the wheel flashed Beta Sydney a quick look and his eyes returned to the road.

"Nervous breakdown," the other Monitor answered. "You're coming back from a stay at Woodbridge."

"When was I supposed to have been first admitted?"

"Two months ago. Your principal had a breakdown, locked himself inside the toilet with his two daughters and threatened their safety."

"Ah," Beta Sydney replied. "I see. So I'm cured now?"

"Yes," replied the Monitor.

Beta Sydney thought for a while. "I guess this episode means that my identity's no longer Grade One?"

The Monitor nodded. "Of course."

"Well," Beta Sydney muttered to no one, "*that's* a relief."

•

They burst into the bathroom door. The force of the blow pitched him forward, and he struck his head on the sink before crashing to the floor. He noticed idly that the blood from his cut was so dark it looked black against the white tiles as blotches formed below his eyes.

Rebecca rushed out of the bathroom and dove into Melanie's arms. He could hear the Monitors shuffling into the bathroom and encircle him. He could see their shoes and their slacks as they gathered around him.

He felt Julie's hand tugging at him.

"Daddy," Julie was whispering.

He felt a needle in his arm.

"Shh, baby," he said. "I'll be okay."

Before he passed out, he could feel them take his limp form onto their shoulders. Had he been awake, he would have seen his wife glare at him as they took him out. Rebecca's face was buried in her arms.

"Mommy, what's wrong with Daddy?" Rebecca said. She should look more frustrated and irritated than worried.

"Don't worry," Melanie said, trying to reassure her. "Everything will be okay tomorrow."

Rebecca looked up at her mother. "He wasn't supposed to do that!"

"I know, I know," her mother replied. She turned to look back into the bathroom and saw Julie crouched in the corner.

"Julie?"

Julie was cowering now, gripping her knees and staring warily at her mother.

•

At the first opportunity, Julie had thrown away the pink hair clips her mother had insisted she wear. Melanie waited in the grocery checkout queue in the Carrefour supermarket in Suntec City. She held a mobile telephone in one hand and Rebecca's hand in the other. Julie had wandered from the counter.

"Don't go far, honey," Melanie had said, not looking up as she punched in an SMS message.

"Yeah," Rebecca snapped with a glare. "*Behave.*"

Julie scowled and made her way into the atrium. All around her, she could see the Sunday crowd busy making their purchases, browsing in stores, going off to some rendezvous, attending to some chore, taking care of some duty. Doing what they were supposed to do. Even the children who passed her by seemed to be engrossed in complaining, in holding their parents' hands or in staring at the displays in the mall.

She wondered whether it was like this everywhere in the world or whether there was some place she could go to which was different.

"Excuse me," she heard someone say.

She turned to face a man dressed in the Carrefour uniform, pushing a line of supermarket trolleys.

"Hello," she answered. Her heart jumped as he pushed the trolley by, the metal wheels and metal siding of the trolleys rattling busily as they moved.

"Wait," she said as he made his way to the ascending escalator near the entrance. "Wait!"

He turned to her. "Yes?"

She paused. "I'm looking for someone," she said.

"Who?" he replied.

"My Daddy," she replied.

"Ah girl!" She heard mother calling.

She was emerging from the row of counters now and making her way rapidly to her. Julie could tell she was angry because she wore that same look when Julie once came home with a D for her math test. Rebecca was trying to keep up behind her.

"How many times have I told you not to go off?" Melanie asked, irritated and reaching out to her.

"She said she was looking for her father," the trolley attendant replied.

Melanie did not look at him and rolled her eyes. "Come, enough of this nonsense!"

Julie turned to the trolley attendant.

"I have to go."

"Okay, bye, girl," the man said suddenly.

Julie stopped. "Goodbye," she smiled.

Beta no more, Sydney had settled in comfortably. It wasn't a Grade One assignment, but it seemed that the original Sydney Wong had done quite well for himself. That made the transition smoother. He was glad, in the end, that HR had refused his application.

Maybe, Sydney thought, he could upgrade his identity to Grade One again.

He drove the car to the pick-up point where he saw Melanie and the girls.

Melanie seemed perturbed as she climbed into the car.

"Not again," Sydney said, reading her thoughts.

Melanie nodded, rolling her eyes.

"Who did she think it was this time?"

"A trolley attendant," Melanie said flatly. "She's such a troublemaker."

"Like father, like daughter," Sydney said, with disapproval.

Video

Alfian bin Sa'at

If not for some last minute changes, Maimon would have been *Hajah* Maimon Binte Putih by now. She would have been able to sit in her living room while passing trinkets to her daughter, her relatives, neighbours even. She would go as far as to offer some of her souvenirs from Mecca to Zainab, who once spread the word that Maimon's husband was a divorcee, as if there was something shameful about that. She would let Zainab have her pick of a *tasbih*, the Muslim rosary with thirty-three beads, or a prayer mat with a tapestry of the Ka'abah. The holy Zamzam water she would store in plastic bottles to distribute to her friends' grandchildren. She would encourage them to drink the water before their exams so that they will be *terang hati*, or have hearts incandescent with the light of knowledge.

The last-minute change was, of course, something that only the rain could bring. Maimon had been awoken by the sound of water on glass, slapping on brick, a sound she had never gotten used to. This was because her earliest memory of rain was the sound of droplets on a zinc roof. "It's raining," she told her sleeping husband, Abu Bakar, as she got off her bed to fasten the sliding windows.

The ceramic tiles were cold against her feet and wet where the wind blew mists of rain into the kitchen. Outside, the trees were swaying darkly, as if welcoming someone's arrival. When Maimon got back to her bed she was sulking and complaining, "You can't even get up to help me." One minute later, with the sound of wind against the walls of her home to drown her sobbing, Maimon realised that there was no way her husband could have given her a hand because he had stopped breathing.

The funeral was a quiet affair; a congregation of slippers and shoes gathered at the door, the female relatives wearing white headscarves taken out of mothball-minty cupboards only for special occasions like deaths, and the male relatives at the corridors, leaning over the ledge to smoke. Strangely, as Maimon was crying, she never once thought of her husband. The only thing that was inside her head was the rain. Why did it come at the same time her husband was dying? And why did it take her away from his side? She should have been there during his last moments, to hold his hand and tell him to think of God, to finish up his sentences for him. She wanted him to know that she would pray for him every day. The rain had been spiteful. It crowded at the windows and pulled the house down into darkness. The moment Maimon knew her husband was gone was when she switched on the fluorescent light and his eyes failed to wince. That sight was something she would carry with her for the rest of her life.

Abu Bakar had married a girl he had met working at a department store when he was eighteen. During the wedding, they had seven costume changes. There was one where she was dressed in a kimono and one where Abu Bakar was done up like an Arab sheik. They also received a swan made up entirely of one-dollar notes. What he remembered most about their wedding dais was the pink satin, not because he didn't like pink but because the girl's mother had insisted on the colour. Two years later, they were divorced.

After that, Abu Bakar held odd jobs, working for a while at the end of a car wash, polishing windscreens, and later as a mechanic in an auto repair shop. He would return home every day with grease under his fingernails. Five years later, his mother decided that it was time for him to find another wife. Through a cousin, she managed to find someone who was two years older than Abu Bakar. The girl was then working as a stacker at the supermarket near her home. Her name was Maimon.

This much was what Abu Bakar told his new wife, and this much was what she lived with for forty-four years of marriage.

One week after the funeral, Jamilah went down to visit her mother. She had moved out of the flat in Choa Chu Kang when she managed to get married at twenty-six to Azhar. Azhar was a man five years older than Jamilah who worked at the post office. Azhar was an orphan. His parents had passed away three years ago, within a day of each other. On some Singapore Post Family Days, he would ask Jamilah's parents to join them. He was childless, and having his in-laws with him on Family Day made up the numbers. After moving out, Jamilah visited her parents about twice a month. Part of it was because she was busy as a leading member of her Community Centre's aerobics group. She was responsible for holding activities like jogging on Fridays and for bigger events like getting people down for the Great Singapore Workout at the Padang, where even the Prime Minister was involved. Part of it was also because when daughters visit their mothers they usually bring their children along.

"*Assalaamualaikum,*" Jamilah greeted at the door. It was Maimon who answered her and opened the door. Jamilah reflected on how, from now on, it would always be Maimon opening the door.

"I've just finished praying," Maimon told her. At this point Jamilah would usually ask if her father was sleeping, and her mother would grumble how the only thing the old man did was sleep. But now there was only silence.

"I bought these," Jamilah said. "When I came out of the

MRT, I smelt them. Quite expensive, ten dollars one kilo. Better be good." Jamilah handed a bag of chestnuts over to Maimon. Then she went to seat herself at the dining table, beside the vase of plastic flowers she had bought from Geylang for her mother.

"You've been cleaning, it seems," said Jamilah.

"I have many things to give away," Maimon replied.

"How about the tickets?" Jamilah was referring to the two tickets for the *Haj* which had been reserved for her parents. They were supposed to have gone in two months' time.

"The agency managed to get people who wanted those tickets. Nowadays it seems a lot of people want to go for the Haj."

"At least the tickets aren't wasted."

"Do you know, I learnt during my Haj course that if you die while performing the pilgrimage you go straight to heaven?"

"I know."

"But what to do? It's God's will."

"All in God's hands," said Jamilah. Then she continued, "God loves *Ayah* more than we love him."

Jamilah had heard that phrase from someone, and she thought that it was an appropriate time to use it. Maimon flinched a little because somehow she heard the statement as: *we never loved him enough*. After touching a petal on one of the plastic flowers, a violet one, Jamilah spoke again.

"*Mak*, do you remember *Makcik* Som?"

Who could forget, thought Maimon. That was her husband's first wife.

"Why?"

"She sends her regards."

"You met her?"

"Yesterday at the market at Hougang."

"What did she say?"

"She said she heard about the death and she just wants to send her regards."

"That's all?"

"That's all."

Suddenly, Jamilah remembered that it was from Som whom she had stolen the line about God's love from. But she kept it to herself.

Maimon had been thinking about this Som woman since her husband's death. There were two things, she thought, where life had cheated her. The first was the rain coming at the wrong time.

The second was Som. Maimon could not bear to think that her grief for Abu Bakar could be shared by another woman who was once his wife too. Who might have even believed that if only Abu Bakar had stayed with his first love he would have lived a little longer. She wondered which of his wives Abu Bakar would choose to accompany him in heaven if God were to let him have only one.

"Look at all this. We were ready." Maimon pointed to some opened suitcases on the floor. There were some books with Arabic words on them. There was also a lot of white cloth.

"He was packing up all this, and every day he asked me when I was going to pack my things. He was excited. I think the old man knew that he was going," said Maimon.

"He had a lot of plans," said Jamilah.

"He said that one of the things he wanted to do when we got to Mecca was pray for you. We wanted to pray for you and Azhar. We know you've wanted children for so long. You've been trying. We know that in Mecca, if you pray and your heart is pure, your prayers are answered."

Jamilah turned away from her mother to inspect the things in the suitcases. Inside her a word knotted itself and grimaced: *enough*. There was an electric shaver, a portable iron, and even an electric heating coil, for boiling hot water. There was also a box which Jamilah opened excitedly. She unwrapped its insides from a bubble sheet.

"*Mak*, he bought this?" Jamilah asked, holding up the video camera.

"Yah. Why?"

"Where did he get the money?"

"Your father was the sort who saved his money. He didn't spend on things like snacks and biscuits."

"How much is this?"

"Nine hundred, I think. If you want it you can have it."

"Wow . . ." Jamilah started to play with the buttons. "There are batteries inside. *Mak*, I can see you from here." Jamilah was peering at the bluish miniature of her mother from the eyehole. "*Mak*, say something."

"Don't want lah, put it away."

"Say anything, *Mak*, don't be shy!"

"You want it you take it. Don't play with it here."

Maimon reached out and took the video camera away from her daughter's hands. She walked into the kitchen and placed it on the table beside a basket that held bananas. Then she walked back into the living room.

"When he bought it, I was really shocked. Nine hundred dollars for that! I asked him, are you out of your mind or what? But your father, he just laughed at me. Then he took out the strap and attached it to the camera. He slung the thing on himself and walked around the living room. He was telling me, it's important to wear it with the strap because when we ride on camels the camera might fall off. He was talking about camels!"

"He was funny, *Mak*. *Ayah* was always funny," Jamilah said.

But Maimon said, "Your father was a dreamer."

It was evening when Azhar got back from work. When he walked into his living room he found his wife watching *The Pyramid*

Game on television while eating chestnuts.

"You went to see your mother just now?" Azhar asked. "How is she?"

"She's well," Jamilah answered.

"That's good."

Jamilah passed her bowl of shelled chestnuts over to her husband.

"She's got a video camera."

"For what?"

"My father bought it for the Haj trip."

Azhar looked at the television screen and munched slowly on the chestnuts in his mouth.

"Is the new host better than the old one?" Azhar asked.

"He's okay."

"The old one didn't look too comfortable in front of the camera. But this one is better I think."

"You know, just now, Mak said I could have her video camera if I wanted it. She wants to give it away."

"You want it?"

"I don't know. It's expensive."

"What do you want to do with the video camera? You want to make a movie? Send to *America's Funniest Home Videos?* Send them one of yourself doing aerobics."

Jamilah looked down into her bowl of chestnuts. "My friend has a video camera."

"But really, Jamilah, what do we need it for? What do your friends use it for?"

"Birthday parties. Holidays. I saw this advertisement once. They said that if you had a video camera you can catch the first time your baby learns to speak, or to walk. We can catch a lot of first times on video."

Azhar looked at the television screen one more time before he walked into the bedroom. Before he went off he said, "They're all the same, all these hosts. He's no better than the previous one. It's a lousy show. Why do you keep watching? You want to see who wins, right? After that, then what? Wasting time!"

The next day Jamilah visited her mother again. When Maimon opened the door she told her daughter, "I was just thinking about you."

"What were you thinking about?" Jamilah asked. "Come in first."

Jamilah walked into her old house and noticed that the suitcases were not around any more. In fact the place looked so neat and unchanged that she had to remind herself that the house had lost half its occupants. The sofa set with its wooden armrests and brown velvety cushion covers was still around. The television still had its crocheted white cover, and on the walls were the two white plates which her parents had bought from a bazaar in Malacca; one reading "Allah", and the other "Muhammad" in Arabic. The cuckoo clock hung above the television set, with its two pendulous handles. And on the floor was the linoleum which had spots of dirt at its edges. When Jamilah was a child, she liked scratching off those sticky bits of compressed dirt.

"Look at this," Maimon said, handing her the video camera.
"Why?"
"What's that red light?"
"Oh, it means ... wait, Mak, you got the manual?"
Maimon gave her daughter the manual which had a Japanese section, a Spanish section, and an English one.
"Oh," Jamilah said after reading the manual, "It means battery is low. You didn't switch it off from yesterday."
"Is it spoilt?"
"I don't know. Mak, do you have the big cassette converter?"
"What is that? I don't know, I just pass everything to you, you take what you want."

"Okay."

After half an hour of reading the manual and trying things out on the video camera, Jamilah figured that she now understood how to use it. While her mother was sweeping the kitchen, Jamilah slotted the video cassette into the player that was on the shelf under the television.

"Don't want lah, put it away."

"Say anything, Mak, don't be shy!"

"You want it you take it. Don't play with it here."

"Smile!"

When Maimon heard her voice, she walked out into the living room to find her face on the television screen. All the wall mirrors in the house had been turned over to face the wall during the funeral out of superstition, and Maimon had never felt the need to restore them to their proper positions. For the first time in a week, Maimon caught sight of her many white hairs and was convinced that her grieving had caused many more wrinkles to appear.

Then the screen showed the camera hovering from the living room to the kitchen. It showed from the level of the dining table: the kitchen cabinets with the Milo tins, the ketchup bottles, and even the woks and aluminium pots on the cooker. The screen was still for a long time. Jamilah reached out to press the fast forward button.

Very soon a figure walked into the frame, and Jamilah eased her finger off the button. The figure was taking out a match to light one of the cooker hobs. It moved slowly, placing a pot over the hob. With one hand, it stirred the things in the pot with a red ladle that was lying on a pink towel on the cabinet. The other hand the figure placed on its hip. Then suddenly, the figure stopped stirring and put both of its hands to its face. The video camera caught what sounded like sobbing. Then the figure pulled the front of its clothes up to its face and the lower part of its back could be seen. Then it continued stirring, faster this time.

When Jamilah turned back to look at her mother she saw the frowning expression on her face.

"That's me," said Maimon. She was leaning on the edge of the sofa, a frail right hand gripping the armrest.

"Yah."

"Jamilah, I have something to ask from you."

"What?"

"Today don't go home so early. Teach me how to use the camera. And also the video player. I want you to teach me."

When Jamilah finally left her mother's house it was already dark. She vowed to herself not to visit her mother so often. She also regretted not being able to bring home the video camera. But she soon forgot all about it as the scent of roasted chestnuts reached her, and the throaty voice of a Chinese man hawked it at ten dollars per kilo.

It had been a month since Jamilah visited her mother. Within the time she had been busy organising a potluck for the members of her aerobics group. She had also managed to lose three kilograms.

Azhar still worked at the post office and sometimes brought home souvenirs like a calculator-cum-digital alarm clock that commemorated his "Ten Years of Outstanding Service". When he showed it to Jamilah she said, "Good, we can use it the next time we go on our honeymoon." Of course as usual Azhar had nothing to say in return.

Within that month, Jamilah never missed an episode of *The Pyramid Game*, although sometimes Azhar pointed out that the people who won weren't going to share their prizes with her. Jamilah also tried each night to love Azhar more than the previous night, but on some nights she would stop. That was when she started thinking of how it would be to video themselves in bed to see what they were doing wrong. There was one night when the thought entered her head and she had to stop suddenly.

She clutched Azhar by his shoulders and told him, "Azhar, we cannot go on like this. Tomorrow I will see the doctor."

Jamilah was ticking off names on a list when the telephone rang. She thought it was going to be one of her aerobics friends but it turned out to be Maimon.

"Milah, when are you coming to visit me again?"

"You want me to come down?"

"I'm just asking. It's been one month."

"I'll come down later today."

"I have something to show you."

In the afternoon, Jamilah took the train down to Choa Chu Kang. When she looked around the carriage, she saw an Indian woman who had her son sitting beside her. He was sleeping on her shoulder with his mouth slightly open.

When Jamilah settled down at her mother's place Maimon made her sit on the sofa while she got out a glass of rose syrup. Maimon then took out the video camera and slotted a video cassette tape into the video player.

"I have been playing around with this thing," Maimon told Jamilah.

"My mother wants to be a director. Can go Malaysia and make movies. Like Yusof Haslam."

"No, you see what I did with it. You just see."

The television screen flickered and then showed the living room. There was no sound except that of passing cars. A vase of flowers appeared on the screen, the plastic violet ones that Jamilah had bought for her mother for Hari Raya three years ago. They were dusty and scentless, but their colour had not faded. The camera panned, and Jamilah recognised the sofa she was sitting on. It was unoccupied.

Video

"Mak, you got nothing to do ah?" Jamilah asked.

Maimon was smiling to herself.

"Last time your father lost his IC. We looked around the whole house, cannot find. But you found it behind the cushion. There. If we lose things in this house it's usually you who can find it. And your father used to say it's because of your big eyes."

The camera moved to show Jamilah's old bedroom. There was a cupboard with one of its hinges broken that was fastened with raffia. A hand appeared to open the cupboard to show yellowed magazine posters of Cliff Richard and Tom Jones pasted on its inside doors. Then the camera moved to reveal the bed. It moved in to show one of its legs, propped up by a folded-up scrap of newspaper.

"Your father loved you. You remember last time, when we had those lucky draw tickets? He always put your name down, even though you were just three years old. Jamilah Binte Abu Bakar. He said you would bring us luck. Then when you learnt to write, he let you fill them up by yourself. Because of that, you always remembered your birth certificate number."

The camera then moved into the kitchen, and it lingered on a shot of the table.

"When you were small, we would put you on the table. You were not so heavy at that time, and you liked to play with the dish cover. You opened and closed it like it was an umbrella. We fed you at this table. But when we went away you started to cry because you didn't know how to climb down."

Jamilah became conscious of her own body and thought how ridiculous it would be to want to sit on that table again. And all those lucky draw coupons. She remembered filling them up, but why had she never brought her parents any luck? There were all these prizes that were promised, three-day-two-night holidays to London, luxury cars, gold watches, whatever happened to all that wishing, all their laughable hopes?

She thought of what a terrible woman her mother was. How could she show Jamilah these shots? What was she trying to do? It all pointed to the fact that a house with no children had no memories. When Jamilah looked at the empty house on the screen, she saw toys spilled onto the linoleum, she heard footsteps, a baby's faraway cry. She regretted coming to her mother's house.

She regretted having a mother, and she regretted not being one. But when Maimon spoke, Jamilah realised that she was the cruel one for having such thoughts.

"When I look at all this," Maimon said, "I know he is around."

Jamilah looked at her mother.

"I know he didn't go to Som's house. He's decided to stay here. He loved me more. He loved us more, you know, Milah. You see."

In the next shot, there was Maimon sitting on the floor, doing crochet. Sunlight was falling in from the windows and bouncing off her spectacles. When her crochet needles moved, they caught the light and sent out glimmers.

"He's looking at me while I'm working. He knows I am thinking of him."

Jamilah reached her hand out and pressed the stop button. Static roared on the screen. Maimon stared at her daughter.

"Mak, I have to go."

At the door, Maimon pressed the video into her daughter's hands.

"Take it," Maimon said. "It's yours."

While walking through the void deck, Jamilah was seized with a sudden urge to sit down. She found a park bench and placed the video camera by her side. She tried to recall why she had not allowed the video to keep on running.

As she was watching the screen, she had sensed how there

were actually four people in the living room. Both mother and daughter felt it and felt themselves shudder with the knowledge. They were watching and, at the same time, being watched, by a child who was not yet born and a husband not yet gone. They were in the company of ghosts.

A cold wind was seeping through the trees. From far away, Jamilah could hear an MRT train urgently pounding the rails. She stood up to leave and left the video camera on the bench. After a few steps, she turned back and switched it on. The video camera whirred and its red light started blinking. On its viewfinder was Jamilah, walking towards the direction of the MRT station, becoming smaller and even smaller.

The Judge

Claire Tham

The woman stood in the supermarket aisle, looking at the judge. Just looking at him, with her prominent, slightly rheumy eyes. In her trainers, she stood barely five feet tall. Her greying hair was square cut, like a man's; she wore a loose worn black T-shirt and black cut-offs that stopped just above her knee, an ensemble that did nothing for her middle-aged, sagging figure. A brown shapeless bag was clutched to her chest.

The judge cleared his throat. "Can I help you?"

She merely waited, her large eyes trained on him. He felt absurdly vulnerable, almost naked, standing there with his hands clamped on the handle of the supermarket trolley, clad in nothing more than his Saturday morning grocery shopping attire of Polo T-shirt, bermudas and Birkenstock sandals. Normally, his wife would have been with him but she was in bed this morning, down with flu. His wife would have known how to deal with this woman; how to manoeuvre her deftly out of the way with the right word, the right gesture.

"Do I know you?"

No, he had not been imagining it, the sensation these past weeks that someone had been following him. He was not an imaginative man—that was why he had gone into the law—but the conviction had grown on him lately that he had a shadow. He felt it as an actual tingling along the spine, a kind of hyper-sensory alertness that made him whip around when he was walking along the street or venturing out in the evening with the family dog. Someone was dancing, darting, at the periphery of his vision: a man or a woman, he could not say. He only had a general impression of a short stolidity, a stolidity that yet managed to be elusive. Troubled, he'd made an appointment with an eye doctor, who'd pronounced the condition of his eyes to be excellent.

Now it—she—stood before him, and his first sensation was one of relief, that he was not losing his mind. His second was one of indignation that anyone could make him doubt his sanity, even briefly, least of all this woman whose very ordinariness seemed to compound her offence.

Still she said nothing, just stood there looking at him with that mild, solemn, almost apologetic expression, as though he ought to know what she wanted. Involuntarily, he took a step back. The judge had not been a judge long, but he had quickly got used to the panoply of unbridled emotions that people somehow felt entitled to give vent to in the courtroom: the rants, the tears, the curses and once, in a scene he would not soon forget, an accused leaping across the aisle to sink his teeth into the prosecutor's forearm. In his courtroom, he had seen just how fragile was the veneer of self-control that kept most people in check. The woman before him had done nothing to make him think she was about to go berserk, but he didn't want to take the risk. There was something about her.

Behind him, an irate voice said, "Excuse *me*," and he turned to give way to a woman hunched over her trolley like a racing car driver. When he turned back, the woman with the rheumy eyes was gone.

It was while waiting in line at the cashier's that it came to him. He had seen her before. He had seen her every day in his courtroom for the past week without registering who she was, because she was the kind of woman who was always in the background (she could have been the auntie who cleaned his office or who manned the cashier at his petrol station) and because, when he was hearing a case in court, he developed a kind of tunnel vision so that everyone other than the accused, the witnesses and the lawyers became invisible.

She was the mother of Wong Yee Oh.

On the morning of September 5th, Wong Yee Oh strapped on his helmet and wheeled his Kawasaki motorcycle out of the narrow alleyway behind the Johor Bahru shophouse where he lived with his uncle, who ran a profitable business selling pirated DVDs to Singapore tourists. His uncle was also his boss. Four years previously, his uncle had shown up on his parents' doorstep in Seremban, Yee Oh's hometown, with the offer of a job, solving at one stroke for Yee Oh's parents the intractable problem of what to do with him. Never academically inclined, Yee Oh had dropped out of school at fifteen and was drifting into a life of petty crime. His father was a mechanic, his mother a hawker stall assistant, and it was the usual story: too many children, too little money and no time at all for Yee Oh, a child somewhere in the broad middle of the family; easily overlooked, always underfoot.

In Johor, Yee Oh had fallen in love, not with a girl, but with a neighbour's Kawasaki motorcycle. Infatuation drove him to apply himself and in three years he'd squirrelled away enough to make a downpayment on his own bike. The day he wheeled it home from the showroom, his uncle testified, the boy's face had glowed. Simply glowed. The care and attention he'd lavished on that bike!—buffing and polishing and waxing it every evening to a high shine that dazzled the eyes just to look at it.

It was the Kawasaki that Yee Oh was piloting across the Causeway to visit his aunt in Woodlands when he was pulled over by Singapore Customs. The Customs officer had pointed to a fine line of white powder trickling across the black gleaming bodywork and down the leg of Yee Oh's jeans. According to the official, Yee Oh had simply said, "Oh." Not satisfied with this answer, the official produced a Swiss penknife and, with one swift movement, slashed open the motorcycle seat at the same time as Yee Oh lunged forward and, shouting in Mandarin, tried to snatch away the penknife before another officer grabbed him, pinning his arms back. From the ripped seat, small plastic packets of a white substance, each about the size of a bar of soap, tumbled out, including one that was torn. The cause of the white powder was explained.

"What's this?" the officer wielding the penknife had asked, holding up a packet. "Drugs?"

"No. I don't know."

"How did it get here then?"

"Someone must have put it there."

The night before the judge's encounter with the woman with the rheumy eyes, Daniel had said, in that lazy, ribbing way he had, "I hear the Wong Yee Oh case is before you, Dad."

At thirty-three, Daniel had the wiry tautness of a gym rat, devoid of body fat. Balding since an early age, he had recently decided to shave off all his hair and sport a pencil moustache. His shirt was black, untucked, body-hugging, with a high accentuated collar. He looked vaguely, disquietingly Mephistophelean.

When Daniel was first born, the judge remembered, he had cried for three nights straight. Screamed, rather, as though he was channelling all the rage his tiny being had felt at being born into the only way of expressing emotion available to him. Daniel had been a clever, intense, sarcastic child, forever asking *why*; less of a question than a gauntlet thrown down to his father, it made the judge long to take him by the shoulders and shake that putting-the-cat-among-the-pigeons-look out of his son's eyes. He never did, of course, but perhaps he should have.

The judge fiddled with his wineglass; he seldom drank except when Daniel came over for dinner, which was not often. He'd forgotten that Daniel was coming that Friday night; his wife had reminded him when he stepped into the house, and there was a beat while he tried to keep the dismay out of his face.

Dinner was Peranakan, Daniel's favourite. *Buah keluak*, assam fish head, *ngoh hiang*, *hee peow* soup; the table groaned under the weight of the food. Bee Ling always cooked too much, pouring all that nervous energy of hers into her cooking as though the production of food could somehow fill the empty nest she faced every day ever since Daniel had moved out years ago.

The judge should not have risen to the bait but he did, perhaps because he had been trying all night, like a car clumsily merging into heavy traffic on the expressway, to find a way into the conversation that flowed easily between mother and son. (And yet, if he'd put his mind to it, he would have been hard pressed to remember what it was that Bee Ling and Daniel had been talking about: the antics of various relatives, celebrities, none of which he followed and had nothing to add to.)

"And how do you know about that?"

"It was in the papers, Dad. I *do* read the papers, you know, Dad."

Did he have to say *Dad* in that way, with that sly, repeated emphasis?

"Well, I didn't see it." Not true: he had seen the article, but avoided reading it. He never read articles about his ongoing cases; he was scrupulous in that respect. "And you know I don't talk about my cases."

"It's not the *details* I'm interested in, Dad."

The judge sighed. "What are you up to these days, Daniel?" As far as the judge knew, Daniel had no obvious means of employment, having chosen not to put to use the law degree from the London School of Economics which the judge had shelled out for. None that counted in the judge's eyes, anyway; Daniel had once been quoted in the papers as a "lifestyle guru", giving his opinion about the interior décor of a boutique hotel. The judge had no idea what a lifestyle guru was, or how this translated into a sustainable income. Daniel never asked him for money, but he could not say with certainty that this was true of Bee Ling.

"Don't change the subject, Dad."

The judge pushed away his plate; he no longer felt hungry. "What do you want from me, Daniel?"

Daniel leant forward, his eyes alight. He was in his element, the judge saw; *this* was why he had come for dinner.

"Is this your second capital case, Dad? Third?"

Evenly, the judge said, "Third."

"Does it ever get easier?"

"Does what ever get easier?"

He waited; it came. "Condemning a man to death?"

Daniel's tone, expression, signified: *strictly in the spirit of scientific inquiry, Dad*. Other men might have been fooled, but not the judge.

It was his fault, the judge was thinking, the way things were between them. In those first few nights of Daniel's life, the judge—though he was not a judge then—had experienced a wave of resentment, born of sleep deprivation, towards the squalling, purple-faced infant in his arms so intense it seemed he was never allowed to forget it.

Bee Ling had put down her fork and was looking from her husband to her son with wide, pleading eyes. "Don't," she said, in a voice so low the judge wasn't even sure she had spoken or who she was speaking to.

The judge laid a hand on her arm. "No," he said. "It never does. Is that what you wanted to hear?" And he was glad, in a way, that it had come to this, because it was back to safe, familiar territory for the two of them, that eternal, ancient conflict that had no beginning and no resolution, because it just *was*.

"I don't know," Daniel said. He looked thoughtful, as though he was giving this question serious consideration, as though it *mattered*, when the judge knew better. He knew his son. "Maybe we should ask Wong Yee Oh what he thinks about your answer."

The judge raised his glass and drained it.

"*Someone must have put it there.*"

On the stand, Yee Oh had repeated this in the monotone of a child asked to explain how he'd come to be in possession of a toy that did not belong to him. A child who did not really expect to be believed but, having formulated a story, intended to stick to it with fanatical illogicality. A frosting of pimples traced a sickle shape across his nose; his hair stood at all angles, as though a manic toddler had been at it with a pair of blunt scissors. His eyes, which were fixed permanently on his shoes, were large and prominent in a thin, narrow face. A psychological evaluation had revealed him to be of average or slightly below average intelligence with no mental impairment. He was twenty-one.

"So are you alleging," the deputy public prosecutor had said, feigning outraged, eye-rolling incredulity, "that this was an elaborate—an elaborate and incredibly stupid and incompetent—arrangement between persons unknown to smuggle heroin to Singapore, to trail you to Singapore and, at the appropriate moment, to steal your bike and retrieve the drugs?" A seasoned DPP, she had a rich, velvety voice; if her voice were confectionery, it would have been a double-layered chocolate cake.

Yee Oh had looked blankly at her, even after the court-appointed translator had translated the question into Mandarin for him. It seemed clear he had completely lost the thread of the question after "alleging".

"No," he said, "I mean, yes—"His gaze had that tentative, wavering, suggestible quality which the judge, an army officer during his national service, had seen so often in the eyes of the more fragile recruits. (Recruit, did you leave your rifle out in the rain? —Yes, sir. I mean, no, sir.— Which is it? —Sir, what do you want me to say, sir?)

"Ms D'Souza," the judge interrupted, forestalling defence counsel, who had sprung to his feet, "please re-phrase or withdraw the question."

In the DPP's face, as she gave a hard look at Yee Oh, the judge could have sworn he almost saw an unexpected glimmer of—if not exactly pity, then something perilously close to it.

"Withdrawn."

In the strict, literal sense of the word—and the judge, being a lawyer, was a stickler for these things—he had not, so far, condemned a man to death. His first two capital cases had been open and shut murders. In the first case, the stabbing of a man in a bar brawl, the killing had been captured on CCTV, and scores of horrified eye-witnesses had testified to the fact as well. In the second case, a man had walked into a police station and confessed, matter-of-factly, to bludgeoning his wife to death. The evidence had been incontrovertible in both cases and the death penalty had been mandatory. *Incontrovertible*, a word the judge was particularly fond of. It meant that he had no choice in the matter, no discretion to exercise. He was off the hook. His conscience was clear.

For thirty years, after a stint in litigation, the judge had been a corporate lawyer specialising in banking and mergers & acquisitions. "That must be exciting," people always said who didn't know any better. In the beginning, there had been some excitement, but over the years he'd wearied of nothing more than money being at stake, of all-nighters being pulled in conference rooms under throbbing fluorescent lights while both sides negotiated over the finer points of three hundred page documents, of venality and greed that were not made any more attractive by being clad in Armani suits. Financially, he was more than comfortable; inwardly, he had begun to hanker for some recognition, the chance to play a larger role in life. So when the invitation came to sit on the bench, he'd accepted it with alacrity though not without some pro forma demurrals (he was out of touch with court procedure, he hadn't argued a case in court in years, but he was assured that it would all come back; it was like riding a bike and you never forgot, and he found that it was true.)

He had been asked, in passing, about his views on the death penalty. In truth, it was not something he had given much thought to; in corporate law, there were few opportunities to consider whether to put a man to death. He had given the usual exemplary answer: if it was the law of the land, he had no problem applying it, and he believed it.

And yet, if that was the case, why did he remember the two men so vividly, out of all the people who had passed through his court? The first accused was not much older than Daniel, a young hothead who had just lost his job as a technician and had a history of violence. He'd had a sharp, fox-like face and a coiled, nervous jitteriness; in court, his right leg had jiggled incessantly below the table, until the judge told him to stop it. The second accused, a heavy-set middle-aged man with a string of convictions for assaulting his wife, was a chain smoker who'd seemed more agitated by the absence of his nicotine fix in prison than his impending execution; his white, fleshy lips had continually made a curious, repulsive fish-like sucking motion as though he were reliving the memories of his last, treasured cigarette.

Neither man had shown much emotion at the verdict (although the young man, the judge recalled, had given a slight smile, as though he'd been vindicated in some obscure way). After all, it was a foregone conclusion and neither seemed the type to expend unnecessary sentiment on their predicament.

The night after pronouncing the young hothead guilty, he could not sleep. In the morning, he had asked his law clerk, casually—or so he hoped—about the execution date. It proved to be a mistake; on the day itself, he'd found it extraordinarily difficult to concentrate on the judgment he was writing for a civil case. He'd heard that executions were usually carried out in the morning, but he did not know at what time and it seemed morbid, and a touch prurient, to ask.

He did not make the same mistake in the case of the man with a mouth like a fish.

"So you did not notice that the seat of your motorcycle had been tampered with?"

"No."

"Yet you say you loved your bike and knew it inside out."

Defence counsel: "Is there a question here?"

The DPP had put up her hand in a graceful acceptance of his objection before moving on in that bored, big-cat manner of hers, like a tigress pawing a guinea pig, "And why did you try to stop the Customs officer from slashing the seat of your motorbike?"

For the first time, Yee Oh had looked straight at her. There was an expression of pained incredulity on his face. "It was my bike."

"And it wasn't because you knew what the officer would find?"

"Someone," Yee Oh had repeated doggedly, *"must have put it there."*

On the Monday following dinner with Daniel, the woman with the rheumy eyes was waiting outside the hotel when he emerged after lunch, standing just beyond the taxi-stand under a frangipani tree. She looked straight at him.

The judge, who had been laughing at his lunch companion's joke, stopped short. Now that he knew who she was, he wondered how he could have failed to notice the resemblance between mother and son; both had the same prominent, filmy eyes, a light grey-brown rather than black, and that same air of life having dealt them a short hand. He took a breath. Yee Oh's trial had been postponed for a week to allow final submissions to be made; a sense of extraordinary reprieve, which he did not care to examine too closely, had allowed him to forget the case for a few blissful hours that morning, and he'd enjoyed his dim sum lunch at the hotel's fine dining restaurant even more than usual. Now the case came rushing back and he wondered how he could ever have thought he was hungry.

His lunch companion, a lawyer of some thirty years' standing, was asking him if he was all right. "You look like you've seen a ghost."

A ghost: yes. He'd looked briefly away from Yee Oh's mother to answer his friend, and when he looked back, she was gone. How did someone who looked anything but fleet-footed move so quickly?

Back in chambers, he asked his law clerk to pull up materials on criminal intimidation for him. The materials were on his desk within the hour and he flipped through desultorily, not really reading. Even as he turned the pages, he knew he was not going to make any accusations against the mother. What would he say? That he had a frumpy, middle-aged stalker? (Though he realised, with a slight shock, that Yee Oh's mother was in all likelihood younger than he was.) He knew how absurd it would sound. He could even hear the mockery in his head: "And are you saying, Your Honour, that this woman can't even occupy the same public places that you do?"

When he closed his eyes, he saw her face so clearly it was as though she was in the room with him and looking straight at him.

Defence counsel had done his rumpled best. Defence counsel was a man who had taken a circuitous route to the law through the police force and at times wore an air of surprise that he was defending those whom he would previously have helped to arrest. Defence counsel, the judge guessed, was being funded by the uncle, the only financially solvent member of the Wong family. With nothing much to work with, defence counsel had laid out the defence. Yee Oh was a creature of habit. Every night he left his motorbike in the alleyway behind his uncle's shophouse; every fortnight he made the trek across the Causeway to visit his aunt. It was im*probable*, but not im*plausible*, that someone familiar with Yee Oh's movements could have used him as an unwitting drug mule. After all, his function was only to plant reasonable doubt in the mind of the judge.

"Are you in need of money, Mr Wong?"

"No."

"No girlfriend, no loans, no debts?"

"No."

"No reason at all to become a drug courier, in other words."

Yee Oh had licked his lips; they were cracked, the judge had noticed, and the tip of his tongue passed repeatedly over them as the day progressed, but he had not asked for any water. "No."

"And isn't it right, Mr Wong, that you would never voluntarily damage your bike in any way?"

Each time he was addressed as "Mr Wong", Yee Oh had glanced involuntarily around the courtroom, as though someone else—his father, perhaps—was being addressed. Clearly, it was not often in his short life that he'd had the occasion to be addressed as "Mr Wong".

"Yes," he'd said, so softly that the judge had to ask him to speak up. "I'd never do anything to my bike."

He glanced hesitantly at the judge, as though seeking an affirmation which was not in the judge's power to give. The judge looked down at his legal pad; there was nothing written there and he had nothing to write, but it was easier than meeting that glance.

It had been a hot afternoon: sweltering. Although the window blinds had been rolled down and the air-conditioning lowered, the heat still pressed oppressively against the windows. More than once, *the judge's fingers had tugged at the collar of his shirt under his black robe, while he thought, not for the first time, about the absurdity of the judicial dress code in this city located on the equator.*

Wong Yee Oh. The name of a three-man law firm. Ha ha ha. There was no-one to share the joke with. He had not realised it before, but the bench was the loneliest place in the world.

On Friday morning, as was his habit, he woke before six, laced up his track shoes and prepared to set out for the stately jog around the estate that was his staple exercise.

The woman with the rheumy eyes was waiting across the narrow street outside his house. Even in the weak lemony light cast by the street lamps, there was no mistaking that dumpy waistless figure. Her outfit was the same as it always was, causing the judge to wonder, distractedly, if she had brought nothing but shapeless T-shirts with her from Johor.

The judge hesitated, wondering if she would follow him if he were to ignore her and jog off; the last thing he wanted was to get into an unseemly chase that would do nothing for his dignity. He squared his shoulders and crossed the street. She stood her ground.

"Mrs Wong, you have to stop this."

She stayed silent. Thinking she might not understand English, he translated it into a stilted Mandarin.

"I can report you to the police, you know."

Still she said nothing. It was an idle threat, they both knew; not worth the breath with which it was uttered.

He had to stop this; he had to put an end to it once and for all. This ridiculous persecution was intolerable. He cleared his throat.

"You have to understand," he said. He paused; his mind went blank. He re-gathered his thoughts; he did not know what he was going to say until he said it: "The evidence is incontrovertible."

He'd intended it to sound judicial yet compassionate; sorrowing yet authoritative. Why then did it come out the way it did, as though he—the judge—were pleading with her?

Manila Calling

David Leo

He was hopelessly in love and desperate, as he sat across the table pleading, "Please help me, Sir. Only you can help me, Sir." He was a small fellow, scruffy, with hair dyed a punky reddish brown. Often I had to remind him to tuck his shirt into his trousers while he was at work. "I must go to Manila, Sir, or I lose my girlfriend." It was a serious matter. Here was a young man, caught in the throes of love, with neither good looks nor social status to his credit—a lowly airport cargo loader. Not that I would venture to guess at his means, as he and his mates were known to be inveterate gamblers, and I had heard stories about how some of them had struck it rich at the lottery, though such tales often came full circle with news of how quickly such fortunes soon dissipated. "I promise you, Sir, this is the last time." He had a poor record of attendance and performance, and his application to consume in advance seven days of leave yet to be earned had been rejected by the departmental manager. "I go to Manila and we get married. That will be the end of all my troubles, Sir."

I remember how he turned up for work one morning wearing a bruised cheek and a swollen eye.

"You got into a fight, Ah Chwee," I remarked.

"I can't help it, Sir, that bastard Filipino man wants to steal my girlfriend."

"You shouldn't mess around with foreigners."

"No messing, Sir. I swear she's really my girlfriend."

Rostia had come to Singapore to work as a maid in a Chinese household. They met one Sunday afternoon at Lucky Plaza where Filipina maids would congregate on their off days for a break from the daily routines of washing, cooking and minding the children. Ah Chwee, who preferred to be called Johnson, claimed that it was love at first sight. "She's very beautiful, Sir, just like a model." From the little that he had told me about the affray, Ah Chwee was fortunate to escape with relatively minor injuries only because Rosita pleaded with her compatriot to let him go. "She really loves me, Sir. I love her also, very much."

That should be reason enough for them to get married. Then came the urgency. Rosita's employer had decided to repatriate her back to the Philippines ahead of the expiry on her employment contract. It was not uncommon for employers to be rid of their maids as soons as they suspected that they had become involved in a serious relationship with the opposite sex. Who knew what they might do during the day when their employers were away at work and they were left alone at home with the kids, who might be sworn to secrecy through threats not to spill the beans on such clandestine affairs? Or what trouble they might bring when matters of passion wreaked havoc? It was every Singaporean employer's nightmare to be surprised by a maid's pregnancy, for which he had stood as guarantor that it would not happen. Ah Chwee had confessed that he had on some afternoons stolen into Rosita's bedroom for some quick, impassioned moments of pleasure. He even boasted that he had a duplicate key to the house. Because he worked irregular shifts, he availed himself of such opportunities quite easily. On the other hand, he couldn't keep constant watch over his paramour on Sundays when she had her break and he had to be at work loading cargo at the airport. That was when he began to fear losing her. He became suspicious to the point of being paranoid and began looking for a quick fix.

"After we get married, Sir, I'll stay in Manila for one week," he explained. "And then I'll come back to Singapore."

"And when will you next see her?"

"Maybe six months later. Can't help it, Sir. She cannot stay in Singapore. It's the law."

"How're you going to keep the marriage going?"

"I agree to send her money every month." He had planned to give her half his monthly wage. "It's only right, Sir, she's my wife. Don't you agree?"

It didn't matter what I thought. Ah Chwee had not come to see me for advice on marital relationships. His request was simple, to allow him to go to Manila for a week so that he could get married. I wished him all the best.

Letter 03 June, photograph enclosed

Dear Sir,

I want to thank you very much for helping me. I got married two days ago. Now I'm very happy. Please see photo. My wife is very beautiful, do you agree? One day I will introduce her to you when you come to Manila.

Johnson

You couldn't but feel happy for a simple man like Ah Chwee even if you had your doubts about the sensibility of what he was doing. Yet why would I not trust his words? The photograph was evidence of a marriage, taken in a church, the couple beaming like any happy newlywed. But then there was so much said about how anything goes in Manila! You can get married any time! And you don't have to be a Christian to book a marriage in a church. Ah Chwee wasn't one, though I wasn't sure about Rosita. I didn't ask him if his act of tying the nuptial knot was supported by any legal procedures or documents. A marriage certificate, I was told, could easily be arranged at a small fee without any legal hassle and formality. I realised that such thoughts were unkind, unfair and definitely condescending, so I chose instead to congratulate Ah Chwee quietly for his feat. More a "Well done!" than a "Good luck!" I must agree with Ah Chwee that Rosita looked most charming in her bridal gown, and the groom himself, attired in a black tuxedo, cut a surprising figure of such neatness, that I'd never once seen in the man. His hair was still reddish brown, but it was neatly combed and parted in old Gatsby fashion. Indeed, it looked like a picture out of a movie magazine.

Ah Chwee did return to work at the airport, as he had assured me, a happy man. While certain things didn't change, as he continued to look his old scruffy self, love indeed had worked wonders on him, for his attendance at work began to show a marked improvement. There were no more requests for unadvised leave on Sundays to keep watch over his girlfriend, strange as you might think it that he had more confidence leaving Rosita alone so many miles away in Manila than in her spending an afternoon with friends at Lucky Plaza in Singapore. That, I could only concede, was the magic of love and the marvel of faith that kept any marriage going. Ah Chwee, as any other person, no matter what his station in life, deserved as much the fair chance to make it good.

They were married in June. By July, Ah Chwee announced that Rosita was pregnant. There was a quiet feeling of jubilation, perhaps more a sense of achievement that he was going to be a father soon. But there was also a new burden loaded upon his shoulders. "I have to send her more money, Sir." He vowed to spend less on himself and requested to be placed in the queue for overtime work, something which he had shunned in the past when he would have rathered spend his time spying on Rosita, if not, actually with her. "Can't help it, Sir. I want to be a good husband and a good father. I love her very much." But someone had to tell Ah Chwee that living from day to day was not the answer. "What happens when the baby comes? You've got to plan long term." For him, the future seemed so far away, almost non-existent. "I think I will go to Manila and work, stay there." It looked like a sensible thing to do. "I can set up a stall and sell food. Maybe chicken rice." A man in love was unlikely to starve as he would do anything. "And my wife can help me." It was good that he was hopeful. He decided that he would quit after he had collected his bonus at the end of the year.

But that was never meant to be. Three months into the marriage and Ah Chwee was back in my office pleading, "Please, Sir, I must go to Manila. It's urgent, Sir." He wanted unplanned leave of another seven days which he bargained quickly down to five, then three. "I must go, Sir, my wife is in trouble." What trouble, he couldn't tell. Not that he wouldn't tell. "I don't know, Sir, I just think that there is trouble." "Have you heard from her?" "No, Sir." That was the problem. Her silence had renewed his old suspicion that some men might have found their way to her door. He did a little investigative work one Sunday afternoon at Lucky Plaza, chatting with some of Rosita's old acquaintances and went away completely consumed by jealousy, anxiety and uncertainty. He discovered to his dismay that the man who had once fought with him over his love interest too had returned to Manila. The timing, if at all coincidental, was much too cruel. The maids upset him even more when they told him that the Filipino whom they knew as John was Rosita's ex-boyfriend before she arrived in Singapore. He was unhappy that she had not told him so, but then he never asked. He became convinced that Jon was the source of his insecurity. Then came the alarming news from a new maid who had arrived from the same province. Rosita had left to work in Hong Kong. Jon went with her. And she'd never been pregnant. It was all a ruse to take advantage of his magnanimity.

Or was it gullibility?

Cynics were quick to chastise Ah Chwee for his obstinate foolishness. He should have known that this day was coming. The advice was for him to stop thinking about Rosita and Manila and get on with his life in Singapore. But it became clear that nothing would stop him from going to Manila. He said he wanted to find out the truth himself. And then what?, asked the cynics. What satisfaction would he derive from affirming something that everyone testified was clear as daylight? Why take a risk which might do him more harm as a consequence, destroying his self-esteem? There was concern that he was risking his life, heading for a confrontation in Manila. His audacity would mark the end of him. No one would know if he were reduced to pulp in a foreign country. But Ah Chwee was adamant about pursuing his elusive dream. He left Singapore although his application for leave was rejected. He was a despereate man in pursuit of a lost love, more than one burning for vengeance. As a matter of course, his services with the company were subsequently terminated on the grounds of his going AWOL, the letter of termination sent to his last known address, a letter that he probably never saw. Yet he wrote, in his usual halting, terse English, to keep me posted, though not specifically about his love life. I chose to treat it as a mere matter of courtesy.

Letter 14 September

Dear Sir,

I am sorry I must come to Manila. I don't think I can go back to Singapore yet. There are many things I want to take care of.

Johnson

The brief note of no more than three sentences was not meant to be a definitve last letter. It had an uncanny ring of suspense, acting as an unitended cliffhanger, leaving the reader at a loss, helpless and anxious. All you could do was wait, wondering while knowing it wasn't the end of the story yet.

I never quite understood why Ah Chwee took the trouble to maintain contact with me. There was no return address—he clearly didn't expect a response. I supposed he only wanted to tell someone his story; he wasn't seeking advice or comments. I was at best nothing more than a passive listener, and that much I was convinced he knew.

The denouement arrived in a simple card some four Christmases after.

> Dear Sir,
>
> Remember me, Johnson? If you come to Manila, please visit me and I will treat you to the best chicken rice in all of Manila—Johnson Chicken Rice. Also, you can eat *halo halo* made by my new wife. Yes, I married again after Rosita left me. My new wife's name is Aida. She's not so pretty but she is a good wife. We already have three children and one more on the way. You must come to Manila and eat my special Johnson Chicken Rice.
>
> Happy Christmas,
> Johnson

The simplicity and brevity were familiar. But this time there was something definitive about the note. It exuded confidence and cheer. There was good news. It came from a man whom many once thought was rash and foolhardy, but Ah Chwee had finally found his place in life, when Manila called, no thanks to the cynics. One dream eluded him, but another had only awaited his pursuit to become a reality. If that was to be Ah Chwee's last letter from Manila, it was a fitting end to what until then appeared to be an unfinished story, whose outcome remained an open verdict because we were afraid to know what might have happened to the protagonist. Indeed, one will never know the twists and turns in the road until one travels on it. Ah Chwee took that road. While he didn't reveal much of the pebbles and stones he stumbled over along the way, it sufficed for me just to know that all was well that ended well.

Much Ado About Crows

David Leo

It was midday when I stumbled upon a black mass outside the Kembangan MRT station. A bundle of feathers, the size of an open hand. There was some movement and a head perked up to reveal bloodshot eyes. Its beak made some effort to open but not a sound was uttered. One leg tucked under its body and the other stuck out awkwardly, it was clear that the bird was injured.

All I did was stand and stare, completely inert. No doubt about it, the little lame bird could do with some help. I felt a collision of mind and heart. This wasn't just any bird; it was a crow. I had to confess: I hated crows.

Indeed, those black birds were a nuisance beyond description. It looked like a justifiable case to campaign for their extermination.

They lined the telephone wires and broke the dawn with their cantankerous caws, such greetings that invariably had you jump out of bed on the wrong side and ruined the day even before it began. As if that's not bad enough, they returned in droves in the evening with a pall of gloom that shut out an otherwise glorious sunset.

They would nest in the mango tree and feed on its fruit just as they ripened, always a step ahead of you, leaving behind a litter of seeds and rotting scraps. They'd not leave the papayas alone either. I might not mind as much if it had been a different species of bird making a feast of the crop.

Being natural thieves, they made swift swipes at food laid out on the kitchen table. Inevitably, their insatiable greed and hunger would lead them to scavenge and mess up the garbage.

They soiled the clothes hung out to dry.

They teased the puppy at meal times and frightened the children at play. Stories of how they pecked at the human eye scared the wits out of parents.

What bullies they were, to be terrorising the orioles, mynas and sparrows. *Those were the real birds.*

My neighbour had complained often about having to replace the TV aerial. It was not an uncommon sight of crows perching on rooftop antenna, consequently breaking them and interrupting the TV reception. "It's costly," the old man grumbled, "I'm a retired man with no income!" As if those birds cared!

So you see, crows had become a national disaster.

Besides, the hideous black bird had long been regarded as an ill omen, an unwelcome visitor anywhere. My grandmother used to urge me to chase it away before it could caw thrice. I had kept the custom religiously. So can you blame me for not liking the crow when its monstrosity stands in the way of any remote possibility of endearment between man and the bird?

Some people who walked by gawked curiously at me, instead of the bundle of black feathers at my feet. The oddity turned out to be me, not the bird. I began to wish that I had taken a different route, breaking the traffic rules instead of heading obediently towards the green man at the crossroads, which demarcated the land between the new Kembangan neighbourhood of high-rise apartments and the mature Frankel estate where I lived. Somehow the crows preferred the latter vicinity because of its wooded area.

The residents took turns to invite the PPD to rid the estate of the pestilent crows, which showed a phenomenal propensity and capacity for multiplying. The uniformed men arrived with their pellet guns and seldom missed, sending the birds diving mercilessly to the ground. But the crow is a smart creature. After the first few shots, the entire flock soon disappeared only to return the moment the PPD officials left, cawing in celebration of their restored freedom. These birds possess such an uncanny sense of timing, which is nothing less than exact. They always know when to swoop down, gate-crashing even before the party begins.

Yet, upon reflection, why did I have to feel apologetic or uneasy about the accidental encounter? It looked like a judgement flawed by incompatible emotions, bordering on insanity, that I should be standing outside the Kembangan MRT station reminding myself repeatedly that the injured victim at my feet was indeed a crow, and that could only mean one nuisance less.

"Go chase those birds away!" I yelled after the dog. It pranced about the yard and yelped frantically, but those black birds weren't in the least intimidated. They remained perched on the fence, cawing mockingly in defiance.

"Go, Toby, go," I shouted, almost with irrepressible glee, "your job's not done till you bring me one, all bloody between your teeth!" Unfortunately, although the silky terrier was known for its speed, it wasn't fast enough for the bold intruders. Otherwise, we might be compelled to contemplate having regal English pies for dinner, something which neither Toby nor I would relish! A *Straits Times* reader had suggested that Singapore might export the meat to feed the millions in China. It might also provide an alternative recipe for the "Finger Lickin' Good" fried chicken franchise. Yet one morning when Toby was yelping at a fledgling and chasing it in the backyard, the mother bird fluttering and cawing noisily overhead, I was screaming my head off to stop the dog. "No, Toby, no, let it go!" I wasn't thinking of the pie; it was the thought of a defenceless infant, an innocent life, that made me forget the bird was a crow!

I decided to leave the broken bird alone and headed home. The green man at the crossroads had begun flashing and I didn't want to miss it, having missed it a few times white contemplating what to do with the poor thing.

Ah, a poor thing indeed! It was a baby, not quite as ugly as the bigger scavengers that we were used to seeing. It didn't have a prominently hooked beak and, upon closer scrutiny, its feathers exhibited a polished sheen. Perhaps the rays of the sun had much to do with the gloss. In its helplessness, the bird looked so pitiably innocent. As I walked on, I turned and looked back occasionally. I saw people avoiding it as they walked by. They didn't look back. They didn't spare a second thought. They weren't curious. They weren't interested. Ah well, nothing could disguise the fact that the bird was still but a crow! And the day would pass, whether it survived or expired.

It might be to escape from the painful reality of life and death that I too decided to put aside any thought of the injured bird to reflect upon what must seem the more important things in our lives. Or rather, the things that were unavoidably an inextricable part of our lives. It was clear that I didn't have to make the crow a part of my life. I was conscious that I had that choice. There were so many other things to worry about, the spectrum as broad as your life was made out to be, from work and family to the mundanities which were no less significant, maybe even more compelling—the leaking kitchen pipe, the defective ballcock that was not rising in the toilet cistern, the broken TV antenna (blame it on the crows), choked drainage and its stench, a broken window and rats in the rafters... Enough to fill a lifetime without the distraction of a broken bird no better than a crow, let alone volunteering to share the hurt it was experiencing.

Only a couple of weeks ago I had an encounter of a different kind when I went to a kindergarten to check out a place for my child. It was near noon when I arrived to see the Principal, who was at that time eating lunch. With time to kill, I amused myself with the highly imaginative drawings executed by the children and posted on the wall. At about half past twelve, the Principal emerged from the inner office. She was stocky, probably in her late twenties or early thirties. It being a Catholic establishment, I had expected the head to be a nun, but there weren't many of those cloistered women left these days. Change must come with time, faster than I could imagine when I noticed that the woman of authority was wearing a miniskirt and black-netted tights, which didn't do much to disguise her muscled thighs.

"It's about a place for my child," I explained.

"We're full."

"I just want to be sure..."

The secretary interjected, "Miss Wong, I told him his child's application was unsuccessful."

"I'm sorry. There's nothing we can do about it." Miss Wong turned to return to her office.

"Please, can we talk?" She gave me a quizzical look. "I don't want to insist that my child should be given a place, but I'd like to really understand why she was rejected."

I had followed her into her office, uninvited.

"You see," I said, "We're Catholics..."

It had been announced that Catholic children would be accorded priority.

"That's the problem with you Catholics," she retorted as she took her place at a huge desk, cluttered with paper and files. "You think as Catholics you have a right of place."

"I didn't mean that..."

I wasn't prepared for the confrontation, so I turned my attention temporarily to what was left of a bowl of noodles on her desk.

"Let me tell you this," she said, "All children are equal. "

I couldn't argue with that. I remembered a huge picture on the wall outside, one that proclaimed, "Jesus loves the little children, all the children of the world. Be they yellow, black or white, they are precious in his sight . . ." They were the familiar lines of a song which my children enjoyed singing. They were words that their innocence taught them to believe without question, words that I had hoped would continue to be their beacons in later years.

"You see," I said, "being Catholic, my wife and I would like our child to be schooled in a Catholic environment." I recalled sitting at Mass listening to the Archbishop's exhortation to Catholic parents to send their children to Catholic schools and not be enticed by the academic excellence of secular institutions. He bemoaned the negligence of education for the soul. I went on to say, "I guess it's the same with a Buddhist or Muslim . . ."

The reference was my mistake.

Miss Wong was quick to rebut. "That's what you think," she retorted. "As you know," she started crowing, "our kindergarten has an excellent reputation for being one of the best, if not the best in this region, and we get all sorts of people vying for places. Religion is immaterial." Indeed, why should it be when through the ages Catholic missionaries were known to have worked among heathens? After all, Jesus came to save not the saints but the sinners.

"But I thought Catholic children would have priority . . ."

"Why should they? I've said all children are equal." I became somewhat irritated with her professed, almost unashamed but clearly ostentatious alleged interest in humanitarianism. I was simply sore when I found out that non-Catholic children whose parents had not the remotest links with the establishment were allocated places instead. "You can expect that every year our kindergarten will be flooded with applications for more places than there are available," she boasted. "So inevitably we'll have to disappoint some people. You're not the only one. We get lots of calls from doctors and lawyers and managing directors of big companies." Well, of course, personal status wasn't something that I could crow about. She didn't reveal if those doctors, lawyers and managing directors of big companies were successful in obtaining places for their children, but I could imagine the register full of their names. The reference was quite obviously intended for a different effect. Her supercilious manner began to rile me and I quickly realised the futility of pursuing the matter any further. While I retreated, she surprised me with an unexpected zest to press on with her opinionated advocacy. It was as if she had had at last found someone with a willing ear to whom she could evangelise. Almost with a vengeance. "Catholics are the worst people to turn to for help," she said. "When I ask for donations, I get excuses like they're already contributing to the church." They probably did; there was always a collection at the Sunday Masses where I had noticed generous donations by several people. Miss Wong went on to proclaim, "But with the parents of other religions, no problem!"

I had heard that some people made generous financial contributions to the schools where their children had been enrolled. Since Miss Wong had led me this far, I thought I might subtly ask if I could be of any assistance. That might rewrite the rules of the game. The response, I gathered, could come in many forms. "We need a new gym." "It would be nice if we could get the children some musical instruments." "Would you know of some bus company which might provide free transportation for an excursion?" "The library is short of funds for new books." "The school is in dire need of some renovation." "The children's toilets are in bad shape." "We need a sponsor for refreshments for Sports Day." "A concert to showcase the children's talents in a big way is the works. It'd be a pity to let it go just because we didn't have the funds. The children would be disappointed." "We need donations, more donations." In other words, money, more money. Since I was no doctor or lawyer or managing director of a big company, I stood up to leave. But I couldn't resist satisfying my curiosity, so I asked, rhetorically, "By the way, pardon me for asking if you're a Catholic yourself?"

It wasn't a fair question. I felt cruel, having asked. She glared at me, and I knew I had to leave quickly.

Indeed, all children are equal. It's a belief you want to uphold and a standard you don't wish to question. But not all birds are equal. A crow cannot take the place of an oriole or a myna. Not even that of the tiny, timid sparrow. But then ... maybe all baby birds, including crows, are the same. No one is born a bully or a thief, everyone is imbued at birth with the basic goodness of character that is so visibly evident in the angelic faces of all babies. What one becomes in adulthood is the product of the environment. The baby crow cannot be any different from other baby birds, except perhaps for its black feathers and the inherited bad reputation of its species.

As I continued to head down the road home, I couldn't forget that challenge of innocence in the eyes of the injured bird as it looked up at me, lying helpless on the heated ground outside the Kembangan MRT station. It was a plea for compassion, and I fumbled inside myself for an answer, not realising that such a virtue could only be expressed in the free, unprejudiced state outside the encasement of a physical form. So long as the sentiment remained trapped in the prison of the body, it was as good as being non-existent.

Only a week ago I was sitting at the Laguna Food Centre by the beach and witnessing a cat preying upon a crow, gripping it tenaciously between its teeth. By then, the bird was already dead.

Overhead, other crows cawed frantically in a call to battle. They fluttered madly about, shaking the leaves of the trees and hanging like a pall of blackness over the predator. More crows arrived and the cat went under a bench. But so long as the cat held on to its victim, the crows wouldn't leave. It was an intimidating sight. A Malay woman who was helping at a satay stall, annoyed by the fracas, threw a slipper at the cat, which fled without its kill. Soon after, the crows dispersed, abandoning the carcass.

So even crows, for all their ugliness and bad behaviour, feel compassion for a less fortunate fellow being. Strange that they wouldn't leave even though the victim was already dead. That's how much they feel for one of their own kind.

I made a quick turn about for the Kembangan MRT station. Two blocks away, I was finally convinced that I had to do something about the injured bird, never mind it being a crow. I walked doubly fast, my heart keeping pace. At the crossroads, I saw some boys crowding around where I had left the bird. When the green man flashed, I dashed across the road. I heard the boys cheering. One of them stood up and began swinging the crow, the bird tied to a string by one leg and spinning like a propeller. It spun at such a dizzying speed that you couldn't tell that it was a bird or figure out what it was, if you didn't already know: it was just a black blob in rotation. The other boys continued to applaud, urging him on.

"Hold it! What are you doing?"

As the boy stopped spinning the bird, the ebony lump slowly revealed feathers, then a head, a beak and eyes that were closed. It dropped with a thud to the ground, lying completely motionless. I stooped down and stared at the boy holding the string, as if frantically searching for the universal childlike innocence in his eyes. He looked a little nervous. The other boys were just as silent. It was a moment of reflection. The bird, now dead and a non-issue. The boys, somewhat puzzled but otherwise unaffected. And me, impotent and defeated.

I heard a woman's voice. "Let's go," she declared. I saw a hand grab the boy as he dropped the string. They stepped away. The other boys followed. I looked up at the woman. She cast me a curious glance. And as the green man began to flash, beckoning them, I heard her telling the boy, "It's only a crow!"

I can't say, though, that I will become more tolerant of the pestering crows that continue to annoy the residents of the estate. If it's any excuse, crows will be crows! Indeed, it is easier casting stones.

Trick or Treat

David Leo

Sam could weave a story in every face that he saw passing through Changi Airport. It was as if more than twenty-five years of routinely checking in passengers for their flights and supervising this function had endowed him with the gift of soothsaying. These people come and go, he'd say quite nonchalantly, and in all likelihood we wouldn't see them again. But they had left with him a repertory of stories that had taught him more about the vicissitudes of life than any book that he had read. Sometimes I wondered if the stories were real or mere figments of a fecund imagination nourished not necessarily by an innate interest in people but ironically by the boredom of work routines and the attempt consequentially to escape from those doldrums. Once in a while, a familiar story surfaced in the newspapers, stoking public interest with the usual journalistic sensationalism, the story usually gory, definitely sexual and almost always tragic, and it was creepy to think that it was one that you had already heard from Sam the day before.

We were watching a line forming for a flight heading for Haadyai.

"Just look at those hungry old men," said Sam, who was not one to disguise his contempt for others.

There were some twenty of the old heads, no doubt about it that they were old, some of them grinning toothlessly, their jaws hanging loose, their shoulders drooping like poorly constructed cheap wire coat hangers and their eyes looking distant and yellow. Every one of them carried over his shoulder an unassuming, small canvas bag supplied by their travel agent. It was the sort of uniformity you expected of school children, and it struck home the painful realisation that life would come a full circle, but without the puerile innocence of those early years.

Sam turned to me, "Can't imagine us standing in line one day when our bones are already giving way, waiting to board the Uncles' Flight to paradise, can you?" Immediately after that, he broke into a wicked guffaw.

Anyone who had worked long enough at the airport knew why the flight was nicknamed the Uncles' Flight, departing Changi Airport at 4.30 P.M. and arriving in time for dinner in Haadyai. It looked like a lucrative business for travel agents, many of them selling a cheap two-night weekend package, departing on Friday and returning on Sunday. Experienced workers at the check-in counters could read those grey men like an open book and were no longer curious about their twilight adventures. Even the sinister DOM jokes that once made the circuit had become stale.

"One of them will not return alive," predicted Sam with uncanny seriousness, his eyes studying the faces of the men intently, like a predator picking its prey. I was afraid to ask which one. Sam was a firm believer in fate. What fate has decided, no man can change. But it was eerie to suspect that Sam somehow had a hand in that decision. I'd prefer to believe that, as in a game of chance, he might well hit it right after several attempts. After all, stories of such misadventures were not uncommon. Even then, the spectre of one chance in a million was enough to put anyone's hair on end.

Ah Long was quite content to be sitting out his evenings with his old cronies at the *kopi tiam* on the ground floor of a block of HDB flats before returning home around midnight. By that time, everyone else in his family would be asleep. Sometimes he wondered if his wife would miss him if he didn't turn in for the night. Indeed, he would have stayed longer at the *kopi tiam* if the proprietor hadn't insisted on locking up. There were evenings when he was left alone with his cup of *kopi-o* and his cigarettes, yawning as he watched the hands of the wall clock at work. Sometimes the rumbustious shopkeeper would tease, "Ah Long, don't you want to go home to your wife? It's late, don't keep her waiting too long!" And when Ah Long snorted in reply, tired of the same old banter, the shopkeeper would laugh loudly, breaking the stillness of the night with the echoes of his bellowing voice bouncing off the walls of the nearly empty *kopi tiam*.

It wasn't that Ah Long particularly enjoyed the company of the other elderly men, but he couldn't think of a better way to while away his time. He was the quiet sort, quite happy to be assured that no one would ask him for an opinion on anything controversial as he sat on the fringe, listening unaffectedly to the outpourings of the more vociferous men.

One evening, Kim Hai was boasting about his amorous adventures in Haadyai. The balding narrator with bulging eyes, big ears and thick lips, got his listeners so excited that they decided to join him on his next pilgrimage. All except Ah Long, who continued to sit aloof on the fringe.

Kim Hai fired the first shot: "What about you, Ah Long?"

"Me?" Ah Long was feeling awkward.

"Yes, aren't you a man like any one of us?"

"Come on, Ah Long, it's time you reassert your manhood!" There was laughter. More like jeering.

"We're old men," said Ah Long.

"Hey, that's not true. I may look old, but I'm still strong. "Tell us, Ah Long, is your wife still satisfying you?"

Ah Long blushed.

"At my age," he said, "I don't think of such things."

"You're wrong, Ah Long, we're men. And men have needs."

That evening, Ah Long decided that he should go home earlier than was his wont.

It was eleven, and the family had gone to sleep. He opened the door to his room gently and crept in quietly without turning on the light. His wife had left the curtains and windows open, and there was enough light from the street lamps to help him move about. He went into the bathroom and looked at himself for a long time in the mirror. Undoubtedly he had grown old. Then he began to realise how ageing could be such an unforgiving process. While still not as bald as Kim Hal, his hair had thinned out tremendously. Even his brows were greying. His eyes had sunk somewhat and his face was bony, and further down, the Adam's apple was a huge walnut bursting from the thin wrap of dry, creased skin. Ah Long unbuttoned his shirt and dropped his trousers, and scrutinised his skinny frame in the mirror. He couldn't remember when it was last that he became conscious of his body as living flesh, and he felt a tingling of new warmth returning to his limbs.

Ah Long stepped out of the bathroom naked. He didn't realise how full and round the moon was until he got to the windows. He stood there for a while, gazing at the ball of light. He remembered how as a child he had always depicted the moon as a smiling face with eyes, eyebrows, a nose and a wide grin. It was always a happy face. He wondered why when asked to insert the moon in a drawing, inevitably he would choose the full circle over the crescent. He couldn't believe, then and now, that it was the same moon at its brightest, in its most pregnant state, at its peak. Ah Long drew the curtains and crept quickly into bed, but he was careful not to wake his wife. He lay very still for a while, listening to his own breathing, as if suddenly conscious that he was drawing in air. Then he turned and put his arms round his wife, very gently and cautiously at first. She stirred. He moved closer, pushing his unshaven chin against her nape.

"What are you doing?" she said, irritated, as she pushed him away.

He rolled to lie on his side, his back to her.

"And why are the curtains closed?"

She got out of bed and moved to the windows, drawing the curtains apart. When she noticed that he was naked, she reproached him. "For goodness' sake, put on some clothes! You ought to be ashamed of yourself. Have you forgotten that you're already a grandfather?"

He remained silent.

She crept back into bed and, as she lay down, asked him, "Aren't you going to put on some clothes?"

He got up obediently and put on his pyjamas. Not long after, Ah Long boarded the Uncles' Flight to Haadyai. He didn't come back alive.

According to Sam, many an old man had died in cheap hotel rooms in awkward circumstances. "Their hearts can't take all that excitement," he explained. On the other hand, those who survived returned home heroes in their own right, complete with renewed self-confidence and lavish gifts of expensive shark's fins and bird's nests for their delighted spouses and relatives.

But not every face that you see at the airport, Sam would tell you, is a happy one.

"Definitely not those two guys," he pointed out to me one day. "They aren't Thai, they're Chinese. From Kunming."

And they weren't old. They looked reasonably healthy, albeit dishevelled and not quite clean. They were asylum seekers, travelling on fraudulent passports and heading for the US. The first leg of their escape took them across the Thai border to Phuket where an underground agent arranged forged documents for their onward journey, transferring at Singapore's Changi Airport. No doubt about it, they had paid a high price for the pursuit of their dreams. And a higher price awaited them if those dreams proved ultimately to be elusive.

"I pity them," remarked Sam. "I really do."

Ge Minliang and Chen Xin were two unlucky ones who didn't make it. They had travelled a long and arduous journey across many borders before they ended up in the Thai port of Phuket where forged documents had been arranged as the tickets to their dreams. Ge Minliang was married and had a young son and aged parents. Life was hard, and he had heard enticing stories about America, the land of plenty. No wonder San Francisco was nicknamed the Golden Mountain by the early Chinese migrants. Ge Minliang was not concerned about a political ideology that was markedly different. All he sought was an opportunity to make it rich, even if it meant starting over and working twice as hard. Each time that he looked at his son playing in the mud, contented as the child might seem, he felt the pain of his inadequacy as a parent and the guilt of succumbing to its helplessness. It was a difficult decision. He had hoped that by going ahead of his family, he would be able to prepare for them to join him in better times. His mate, Chen Xin, was a bachelor, but that didn't make the choice to bolt any less onerous and painful. By the time they arrived at Changi Airport, all they had left were the clothes that they were wearing.

Their nervousness gave the game away. They had no luggage, which aroused suspicion. Overwhelmed with fatigue, they couldn't offer honest answers to the simple questions asked of them. They broke down under close scrutiny and were classified as inadmissible passengers to be repatriated back to where they last came from in accordance with the international aviation regulations.

Ge Minliang and Chen Xin pleaded not to be sent back to Phuket.

They were escorted to the boarding gate by armed policemen.

Sam had the rest of the story. "Those men know what awaits them in Phuket," he said. "As soon as they arrive at the airport, someone will come and claim them. No big deal. And then they'll never be heard of again. "

I looked at Sam in disbelief.

"Life's cheap there, " he explained. "Besides, these men are like reject goods returned to the factory. They no longer have any value. They've become a liability. So what do you do with them if you don't want to be saddled with the problem of having to continue accommodating and feeding them? You can be sure that the contract doesn't provide for this obligation. It's a cold business decision. More importantly, you don't want them to spill the beans, do you?"

Sam put his index finger to his temple and cocked his thumb. Click! He winked. I was petrified.

Sam grinned, then said, "You might say that those men gambled with their lives and lost."

But, much as he believed in the decree of fate, Sam would tell you in the same breath that life's a gamble anyway. Of course, everyone who gambles, gambles to win. One can choose to ignore the risk of losing, but you cannot refute that it is possible and probable. Then again, if one's fortune or misfortune is dependent upon the whims of fate, chance doesn't quite figure in the outcome which has been pre-determined. For Sam, the conflict is self-inflicted and an innate part of the human psyche: you think you can work at winning, even in a game of chance, but you will seek consolation in fate when woe befalls you.

Sam drew my attention to three seemingly happy faces at the check-in counter one afternoon.

"Ménage à trois," he said, putting on an uncomfortable foreign accent.

"What do you mean?" I asked.

"Can't you even guess?"

My ignorance vexed him.

"Well, there's an old man and a much younger couple. What do you think their relationship is?"

"Don't tell me, Sam..."

He smirked.

"I refuse to believe that..." I said and broke into a chuckle.

There was much chitchatting and laughter among the three passengers. I had never seen a man grinning so blithely in the autumn of his life. His perennial plastered smile revealed a full set of porcelain white dentures and accentuated the protrusion of his pointed chin. He was impeccably attired, wearing a fashionable felt hat that matched his suit. The younger man was causally groomed, looking somewhat clumsy in his Texan blue jeans and boots. The woman was decorated with much make-up and bedecked with jewels. As they turned to leave, the woman placed her arm round the waist of the old man, her crimson nails digging into his jacket and creasing it. Sam looked at me, cynicism hanging from the corners of his lips, and gave me that "now you know" wink.

It was a sensational tale peppered with sex, greed and conspiracy. Joo and Lily, once married to each other, met again after a separation of some five years through a common benefactor at a karaoke lounge where Uly hosted men at tables. By then, old man Pock had recognised Lily as some sort of goddaughter and showered her lavishly with gifts and money. Quite by chance, Joo who was hopping from job to job and experiencing many dry spells of unemployment between odd jobs, became Pock's personal chauffeur and very quickly graduated from driver to personal assistant. One might say that he had found his pot of gold, as did Lily, helping the old man to dispense his largesse. Very little was known about Pock and how he had amassed his fortune.

Strange as it might seem, the threesome got on so well with each other that they all soon lived together in the old man's apartment. Neighbours claimed they knew nothing or too little about them to comment, some of them not surprisingly mistaking the two men for father and son.

Trips to Thailand were frequent. Always the three of them together.

The revelry had to end some day.

The old man was found dead in the bathtub in a room of a cheap, sleazy hotel in a little known part of northern Thailand. He was reported to have died from a heart attack. The young couple were out shopping and were devastated when they returned to collect him for dinner. Apparently he had felt tired and declined to join Joo and Lily in a hunt for excellent bargains in antiques and gems as touted by a local guide. The death was duly reported to the police and the body was cremated almost immediately thereafter in accordance with Buddhist rites. Lily returned to Singapore dressed in black, a silk scarf hiding her hair but not the jewellery round her neck, the urn of ashes pressed against her breast. Joo looked morose when the media confronted them.

The story didn't end there, as Sam would have predicted. Busy days lay ahead for the courts as the parties concerned battled over insurance pay-outs and raised the questions of conspiracy and murder.

"You can tell the story any way you like," said Sam, "but the end is always the same." He never failed to amuse me with some philosophical reflection as he concluded a tale, sometimes speaking more to himself than his listeners. "You might say that the young woman was the bait to squeeze the old man dry, but he chose to bite. Who's to say that he didn't live his life to the fullest? He might have still been grinning when they found him in the bathtub!" I could imagine that, that plastered smile that I saw stretched from ear to ear when he checked in with his mates. It looked like it was stitched permanently to his face. But it definitely spoke of good times. Indeed, few people are said to have died smiling. "Come to think of it," ruminated Sam, "Weren't they baiting each other in his or her own way? Among them, each must have had something that one of the others or both of the others need. Don't ask me what. I guess that's how a ménage à trois works."

I added, "Or you might say that it can all be attributed to fate."

Sam looked straight into my eyes, scaring me. "Yes, fate," he said very seriously. "You might say it's that."

Deep in the wells of his eyes was as much mystery as there were riddles in his stories. I couldn't claim to know him well enough. He told tales of many people but spoke little of himself. From the little that I'd heard about him, he had been living alone ever since his divorce after a short marriage. His ex-wife, who also worked at the airport, had gone to bed with another man. It must have been hard on him. But, outwardly, he looked a reasonably satisfied person, hardly complaining about the low points, if any, in his life. Like most of his male colleagues, he travelled often to Thailand, but I was told that it was with a purpose. He was planning a retirement in Chiangmai, where the weather was clement throughout the year, the pace of life much slower and the people most congenial. The lure, of course, was an enchanting woman who had vowed to bring happiness to his autumnal years. I shall shun the word "bait" which he had employed in one of his tales.

Needless to say, when Sam retired and left the company, I missed his tales about the people passing through Changi Airport. No one else was as blessed with his gift of narration and extra sensory perception. He collected his CPF savings, packed his suitcases and left Singapore for Chiangmai where his love interest had been waiting faithfully all those years that he had known her, visiting her twice or thrice annually for short spells of earthly bliss. It was a love nest that he had constructed and furnished through consistent contributions, sending her large sums of money every month for upkeep. By the time that he was ready to make it his permanent home, she was living in the biggest and most luxuriously furnished house in the small town, much to the envy and admiration of the local folks. He didn't mind that her large family had moved in with her; it was to be a family that he never had and wished he had.

I don't know how much that was told about Sam in his final days by the small circle who knew him was made up and exaggerated, but, as he himself had once said, it didn't matter how the story was told, invariably the ending remained unchanged. If I had been on duty the day Sam arrived to check in for his flight to Chiangmai, I believe I might see as smiling a face as of anyone who was heading for a lifelong vacation in paradise. But because I wasn't Sam, the story might have ended there on a happy note.

It soon became clear to Sam that while absence makes the heart grow fonder, familiarity breeds contempt. It's that dichotomy of the same value that he had often attributed to the natural conflict of being human. The short visits had brought more pleasurable times than a lifelong commitment to living together. It wasn't him, but the other party. For the first time, he realised how very young she was compared to him. And how different they had become if ever they were anywhere near being alike in the past. How little they understood each other. She began to tire of him and became reluctant to wait on him. Then came the revelation that, unknown to him, she had married a young man from the same province, a soldier who would be returning home soon. She pleaded with Sam to leave, or her husband would kill him. Sam knew that anything and everything was possible in that part of the world. So he came home to Singapore, penniless and with two suitcases of old clothes.

I never saw Sam again after he left the company. I heard that he fell ill soon after he returned to Singapore and death mercifully followed quickly. Some people who told his story made the cruel remark that there was no fool like an old fool. It saddened me. Sam was the storyteller who told many tales but kept his hidden in the cupboard, and others not quite as talented found pleasure only in dragging out the skeletons for misplaced sympathy and knowing humiliation. In many ways, Sam was not unlike the characters in his stories, and his personal tale was no less tragic. I wondered if he too had gambled and lost, or that he knew there was no escape from the clutches of fate.

Notes

p. 21 *sotong*: The Malay word for squid.

p. 22 *lontong*: Sliced rice roll served with a coconut-based vegetable stew, a popular dish in Indonesia, Malaysia, and Singapore.

p. 22 *mee rebus*: An egg noodle dish popular in Indonesia, Malaysia, and Singapore.

p. 22 *adik*: A Malay term referring to a younger sibling.

p. 25 *kadi*: An Islamic judge.

p. 25 *Sah*: The Malay word for "valid" or "in order."

p. 25 *bumboat*: A boat that ferries supplies to large vessels lying offshore or in port.

p. 29 *kaya*: A jam made from coconuts and eggs and enjoyed in Malaysia and Singapore.

p. 29 *Milo*: A milk beverage made with chocolate and malt.

p. 29 *Mak*: A Malay form of address to one's mother.

p. 29 *sayang*: The Malay word for love, used as a term of endearment.

p. 34 *tuckshop*: A term from the British colonial era that refers to a shop selling pastries, sweets, soft drinks and the like. In Singapore, it traditionally refers to a school canteen/cafeteria.

p. 35 *A&W*: The first fast-food chain in Singapore, which operated from 1966 to 2005.

p. 44 *IMM*: International Merchandise Mart, a large shopping mall in the west of Singapore.

p. 44 *Johnson duck*: A famous brand of roast duck in Singapore.

p. 44 *bak chor mee*: Noodles with minced meat.

p. 45 *HDB*: Housing Development Board, the governmental

statutory board responsible for public housing in Singapore. As of 2010, 84% of the country's population live in residential blocks built by the HDB.

p. 50   *MRT*: Mass Rapid Transit, Singapore's train system.

p. 51   *C ward*: The cheapest of five classes of hospital wards available in Singapore.

p. 55   *nasi lemak*: Rice cooked in coconut cream and traditionally served on banana leaves with dried anchovies, roasted peanuts, hard-boiled eggs, cucumber slices, and sambal sauce. This is a popular dish in Malaysia and Singapore.

p. 55   *Perhentian*: The Perhentian Islands, situated off the coast of north-eastern Malaysia.

p. 62   *fifteen grammes of heroin*: Under Singapore's Misuse of Drugs Act of 1973, anyone caught with this amount or more faces a mandatory death penalty. This means that the judge has no discretionary power to consider other circumstances before sentencing an offender to death. The amount for morphine is twenty-eight grammes or more, and the amount for marijuana is from 480 grammes.

p. 67   *wasted*: In Singaporean English, used in the sense of squandered potential or lost opportunity.

p. 71   *Kor*: The Hokkien term of address for one's older brother.

p. 74   *tsunami*: A huge sea wave caused by an earthquake or an underwater volcanic eruption. The one in this story is based on the Indian Ocean tsunami, which occurred on 26 December 2004 and resulted from a Sumatran quake measuring around 9.2 on the Richter scale. It ranks among the worst natural disasters known in human history, having killed nearly 230,000 people in fourteen countries. In Phuket, official records put the figures at 259 people dead, 1,111 injured, and 700 missing.

p. 76   *Garuda*: A large part-eagle, part-human creature found in Hindu and Buddhist mythology.

Telltale

p. 77   *National Service*: Male citizens and second-generation permanent residents of Singapore are required by law to serve in the army, the police, or the civil defence corps. The specific reference here is to a two-year period of full-time service that begins from the age of eighteen.

p. 89   *pedicab*: A type of tricycle with hooded seats for passengers often seen in South, Southeast, and East Asia.

p. 96   *SBS*: Singapore Bus Services, the largest public bus operator in Singapore.

p. 96   *two is enough*: The slogan for a state-initiated birth-control campaign that took place in Singapore in the 1970s.

p. 97   *bandung*: A drink in Malaysia and Singapore that is made with milk and rose syrup.

p. 113   *QX plate*: A car plate used by law enforcers in Singapore.

p. 114   *Woodbridge*: Woodbridge Hospital, an institution for the mentally ill in Singapore.

p. 118   *Hajah*: A title for a Muslim woman who has made her pilgrimage to the Islamic holy city of Mecca.

p. 118   *Ka'abah*: A cube-shaped structure in Mecca that is considered the holiest site in Islam.

p. 118   *holy Zamzam water*: Water from a sacred well near the Ka'abah.

p. 120   *Singapore Post*: The main provider of postal services in Singapore.

p. 120   *Great Singapore Workout*: A state-led fitness routine to get Singaporeans to stay healthy through regular exercises. This specific reference is to the campaign's launch in 1993, during which then Prime Minister Goh Chok Tong led a mass jog from the National Stadium to the Padang. It was followed by an aerobics session with 26,107 participants, a crowd so big that it set the Guinness World Record for such an activity.

Notes

p. 120 *Padang*: An open field in Singapore that hosts numerous sporting and large-scale national events.

p. 120 *Assalaamualaikum*: An Islamic greeting meaning "Peace be upon you".

p. 120 *Haj*: A pilgrimage to Mecca that every able-bodied Muslim must make at least once in his or her lifetime.

p. 121 *Ayah*: A Malay form of address to one's father.

p. 121 *Makcik*: A Malay term for aunt.

p. 123 *The Pyramid Game*: Singapore's short-lived version of the American television game show *Pyramid* (originally *The $10,000 Pyramid*).

p. 128 *Yusof Haslam*: A successful filmmaker in Malaysia.

p. 128 *Hari Raya*: Or Hari Raya Puasa, a festive celebration of the end of Ramadan, the Islamic holy month of fasting.

p. 129 *IC*: Or NRIC, National Registration Identity Card. This is the document of identification used in Singapore and possessed by every citizen or permanent resident who is fifteen or older.

p. 136 *buah keluak*: A staple Singaporean dish consisting of chicken or pork pieces cooked with black nuts from the *Pangium edule* or *keluak* tree.

p. 136 *ngoh hiang*: A popular dish sold in hawker centres, consisting of rolls of minced pork and seafood wrapped in deep-fried bean curd.

p. 136 *hee peow*: fish-maw soup.

p. 138 *DPP*: Director of Public Prosecutions, a title given to the public prosecutors of many current and former territories of the Commonwealth of Nations.

p. 152 *halo halo*: A Filipino dessert dish, consisting of a mixture of shaved ice, evaporated milk, and other sweets and fruits.

p. 156 Straits Times: One of Singapore's oldest English-language daily newspapers, founded in 1845.

p. 166   *kopi tiam*: A traditional Southeast Asian coffee shop/café.

p. 166   *kopi-o*: Strong black coffee with sugar.

p. 173   *CPF*: Central Provident Fund. This refers to a compulsory savings scheme begun in 1955 to provide social security for working Singaporeans. The fund takes a part of each worker's monthly wages and allows him or her to withdraw the full, accumulated sum only upon retirement.

Acknowledgments

The editor and publisher are grateful for permission to include the following copyright material:

Alfian bin Sa'at. "Birthday." *Corridor: 12 Short Stories*. Singapore: SNP Editions, 1999.

Alfian bin Sa'at. "Thirteen Ways of Looking at a Hanging." Previously unpublished, 2013.

Alfian bin Sa'at. "Video." *Corridor: 12 Short Stories*. Singapore: SNP Editions, 1999.

Dave Chua. "The Drowning." Previously unpublished, 2013.

David Leo. "Manila Calling." *News at Nine*. Singapore: Ethos Books, 2003.

David Leo. "Much Ado About Crows." *News at Nine*. Singapore: Ethos Books, 2003.

David Leo. "Trick or Treat." *News at Nine*. Singapore: Ethos Books, 2003.

Jeffrey Lim. "Haze Day." *The Coffin that Wouldn't Bury and Other Stories*. Singapore: Ethos Books, 2008.

Jeffrey Lim. "Understudies." *The Coffin that Wouldn't Bury and Other Stories*. Singapore: Ethos Books, 2008.

Acknowledgments

Tan Mei Ching. "In the Quiet." *Crossing Distance*. Singapore: EPB Publishers, 1995.

Claire Tham. "The Judge." Previously unpublished, 2013.

Contributors

ALFIAN BIN SA'AT was educated at Raffles Institution, Raffles Junior College, the National University of Singapore, and the Nanyang Technological University. He published his first critically acclaimed collection of poetry, *One Fierce Hour*, in 1998 and his first collection of fiction, *Corridor: 12 Short Stories*, the following year. *Corridor* won a Singapore Literature Prize Commendation Award in 1999, and seven stories from it were later adapted for television.

In 2001, Alfian published his second collection of poetry, *A History of Amnesia*, which was shortlisted for a Kiriyama Asia-Pacific Book Prize. He won both the Singapore Press Holdings-National Arts Council Golden Point Award for Poetry and the National Arts Council Young Artist Award for Literature the same year. Alfian has received six nominations so far in the category for Best Script at the *Life!* Theatre Awards and won this award twice. He is currently the Resident Playwright of the theatre group, W!LD RICE.

DAVE CHUA was born in Malaysia and came to Singapore at the age of ten. He was educated at Dunman High School and Victoria Junior College and studied electrical engineering and computer science at the University of California, Berkeley. His short story, "Father's Gift", won a Singapore Press Holdings-National Arts Council Golden Point Award in 1995. His first novel, *Gone Case*, was given a Singapore Literature Prize Commendation Award in 1996 and was published the same year.

Chua was involved in the production of the Mediacorp sitcom, *Achar!*, and PeachBlossom Media's animated children's show, *Tomato Twins*. He writes for various publications such as *The Straits Times*, *BigO*, and *The Edge* and is the Vice Chairman of the Singapore Film Society. For his feature-length scripts, he was awarded a second prize at the Singapore Screenplay Awards in 2001. He is currently working on a book of short stories and a graphic novel adaptation of *Gone Case* with the artist Koh Hong Teng.

DAVID LEO has produced a wide repertoire of works that include poetry and prose. He was awarded the Publisher's Prize for fiction (*Ah . . . the Fragrance of Durians & Other Stories*), NB-DCS commendation (*The Sins of the Fathers & Other Stories*) and Singapore Literature Prize commendation (*Wives, Lovers and Other Women*). A fourth collection of short stories (*News at Nine*) is a recommended secondary school text. Between books, Leo writes commentaries on a wide range of subjects but specialises in aviation and customer service as a freelance columnist. He enjoys travelling, swimming and word puzzles. A nature lover, he abhors cruelty to animals.

JEFFREY LIM was educated at Raffles Institution and Raffles Junior College and read law at the University of Bristol. He was a practising lawyer for ten years before becoming an in-house lawyer with a multinational corporation. His first book, *Faith and Lies*, was a collection of seventeen short stories published in 1999. It centres on the thematic duality of fiction and myth, which ranges from the deceptive and fantastic to the redemptive and inspirational. His second collection, *The Coffin That Wouldn't Bury* (2008), brings together twenty short stories written loosely around moments of pivotal intermission in the lives of individuals.

Lim has also contributed short stories to various literary anthologies and collections. His story "News Four" appeared in *Silverfish New Writing 5* in 2005, and "Criticism" was included in *Don't Judge a Book By Its Cover: aka Dead People, Flying Fishes and the Ones who Missed the Boat* (2003). He is currently working on a children's book, a third collection of short stories, and a novel. Lim is married and has two children and two dogs.

TAN MEI CHING holds a Bachelor of Arts in English from Willamette University and a Master of Fine Arts in Creative Writing from the University of Washington. Her first novel, *Beyond the Village Gate*, was given the Singapore Literature Prize Commendation Award in 1992 and published in 1994. Her collection of short stories, *Crossing Distance*, won the Singapore Literature Prize Merit Award in 1994 and was published the following year. This collection also received a Commendation Award from the National Book Development Council of Singapore in 1996. In 1997, Tan received the National Arts Council Young Artist Award for Literature. Her travel narrative, *Towards the Blue: Adventures of a City Wimp*, was published in 2007.

Tan's short stories have won first prizes in the United States and were published in journals there. The short story, "Never Mind Father", was included in *More Than Half the Sky: Creative Writings by Thirty Singaporean Women* (1998). "Release" was included in *Island Voices: A Collection of Short Stories from Singapore* (2007), and "Sunny-Side Up" was featured in *Asian Women's Writings* (2009), published by Penguin India. "The Running Game" reappeared in *Writing Singapore: An Historical Anthology of Singapore Literature* (2009). "Candle, Candle, Burning Bright" will be published in *ALIA: The Archipelago of Fantastic* in 2010.

CLAIRE THAM was educated at the Convent of the Holy Infant Jesus, Hwa Chong Junior College, and Oxford University. A lawyer by profession, she published her first collection of short stories, *Fascist Rock: Stories of Rebellion*, in 1990. It won her a Commendation Award for Fiction from the National Book Development Council of Singapore in 1992. The story "Lee" was adapted for television as a part of a three-episode drama series, *AlterAsians*, produced by MediaCorp in 2000. It was also included in the anthology, *Ties that Bind*, published by the National Library Board in 2007.

Tham's second collection, *Saving the Rainforest and Other Stories* (1993), received a Highly Commended Award from the National Book Development Council of Singapore in 1995. Her first novel, *Skimming*, saw print in 1999. She received Golden Point Awards for two short stories, "The Gunpowder Trail" and "Driving Sideways", in the Singapore Press Holdings-National Arts Council Short Story Writing Competitions of 1999 and 2001 respectively. Both of these stories were included in her third collection, *The Gunpowder Trail and Other Stories*, published in 2003.

GWEE LI SUI is a literary critic, a poet, and a graphic artist. He was educated at Anglo-Chinese Secondary School, Anglo-Chinese Junior College, and the National University of Singapore. He then pursued his doctorate in literature at Queen Mary, University of London, and returned to lecture at the National University of Singapore for a number of years. Topics he has written on include the Reformation, early modern science, the Enlightenment, European Romanticism, German idealism, Protestant theology, modern German literature, and literary theory.

In the area of Singaporean literature, Gwee has contributed several important articles on aspects of its poetic history up to the present. He was the editor of the volume of critical essays, *Sharing Borders: Studies in Contemporary Singaporean-Malaysian Literature II* (2009). Gwee also wrote Singapore's first full-length graphic novel, *Myth of the Stone*, back in 1993 and published a volume of humorous verse, *Who Wants to Buy a Book of Poems?*, in 1998. His poems have been featured in a number of anthologies and literary journals, and his drawings are much sought after.

SELECTED DALKEY ARCHIVE TITLES

MICHAL AJVAZ, *The Golden Age.*
  The Other City.
PIERRE ALBERT-BIROT, *Grabinoulor.*
YUZ ALESHKOVSKY, *Kangaroo.*
FELIPE ALFAU, *Chromos.*
  Locos.
IVAN ÂNGELO, *The Celebration.*
  The Tower of Glass.
ANTÓNIO LOBO ANTUNES, *Knowledge of Hell.*
  The Splendor of Portugal.
ALAIN ARIAS-MISSON, *Theatre of Incest.*
JOHN ASHBERY AND JAMES SCHUYLER,
  A Nest of Ninnies.
ROBERT ASHLEY, *Perfect Lives.*
GABRIELA AVIGUR-ROTEM, *Heatwave
  and Crazy Birds.*
DJUNA BARNES, *Ladies Almanack.*
  Ryder.
JOHN BARTH, *LETTERS.*
  Sabbatical.
DONALD BARTHELME, *The King.*
  Paradise.
SVETISLAV BASARA, *Chinese Letter.*
MIQUEL BAUÇÀ, *The Siege in the Room.*
RENÉ BELLETTO, *Dying.*
MAREK BIEŃCZYK, *Transparency.*
ANDREI BITOV, *Pushkin House.*
ANDREJ BLATNIK, *You Do Understand.*
LOUIS PAUL BOON, *Chapel Road.*
  My Little War.
  Summer in Termuren.
ROGER BOYLAN, *Killoyle.*
IGNÁCIO DE LOYOLA BRANDÃO,
  Anonymous Celebrity.
  Zero.
BONNIE BREMSER, *Troia: Mexican Memoirs.*
CHRISTINE BROOKE-ROSE, *Amalgamemnon.*
BRIGID BROPHY, *In Transit.*
GERALD L. BRUNS, *Modern Poetry and
  the Idea of Language.*
GABRIELLE BURTON, *Heartbreak Hotel.*
MICHEL BUTOR, *Degrees.*
  Mobile.
G. CABRERA INFANTE, *Infante's Inferno.*
  Three Trapped Tigers.
JULIETA CAMPOS,
  The Fear of Losing Eurydice.
ANNE CARSON, *Eros the Bittersweet.*
ORLY CASTEL-BLOOM, *Dolly City.*
LOUIS-FERDINAND CÉLINE, *Castle to Castle.*
  Conversations with Professor Y.
  London Bridge.
  Normance.
  North.
  Rigadoon.
MARIE CHAIX, *The Laurels of Lake Constance.*
HUGO CHARTERIS, *The Tide Is Right.*
ERIC CHEVILLARD, *Demolishing Nisard.*
MARC CHOLODENKO, *Mordechai Schamz.*
JOSHUA COHEN, *Witz.*
EMILY HOLMES COLEMAN, *The Shutter
  of Snow.*
ROBERT COOVER, *A Night at the Movies.*
STANLEY CRAWFORD, *Log of the S.S. The
  Mrs Unguentine.*
  Some Instructions to My Wife.
RENÉ CREVEL, *Putting My Foot in It.*
RALPH CUSACK, *Cadenza.*
NICHOLAS DELBANCO, *The Count of Concord.*
  Sherbrookes.
NIGEL DENNIS, *Cards of Identity.*

PETER DIMOCK, *A Short Rhetoric for
  Leaving the Family.*
ARIEL DORFMAN, *Konfidenz.*
COLEMAN DOWELL,
  Island People.
  Too Much Flesh and Jabez.
ARKADII DRAGOMOSHCHENKO, *Dust.*
RIKKI DUCORNET, *The Complete
  Butcher's Tales.*
  The Fountains of Neptune.
  The Jade Cabinet.
  Phosphor in Dreamland.
WILLIAM EASTLAKE, *The Bamboo Bed.*
  Castle Keep.
  Lyric of the Circle Heart.
JEAN ECHENOZ, *Chopin's Move.*
STANLEY ELKIN, *A Bad Man.*
  *Criers and Kibitzers, Kibitzers
  and Criers.*
  The Dick Gibson Show.
  The Franchiser.
  The Living End.
  Mrs. Ted Bliss.
FRANÇOIS EMMANUEL, *Invitation to a
  Voyage.*
SALVADOR ESPRIU, *Ariadne in the
  Grotesque Labyrinth.*
LESLIE A. FIEDLER, *Love and Death in
  the American Novel.*
JUAN FILLOY, *Op Oloop.*
ANDY FITCH, *Pop Poetics.*
GUSTAVE FLAUBERT, *Bouvard and Pécuchet.*
KASS FLEISHER, *Talking out of School.*
FORD MADOX FORD,
  The March of Literature.
JON FOSSE, *Aliss at the Fire.*
  Melancholy.
MAX FRISCH, *I'm Not Stiller.*
  Man in the Holocene.
CARLOS FUENTES, *Christopher Unborn.*
  Distant Relations.
  Terra Nostra.
  Where the Air Is Clear.
TAKEHIKO FUKUNAGA, *Flowers of Grass.*
WILLIAM GADDIS, *J R.*
  The Recognitions.
JANICE GALLOWAY, *Foreign Parts.*
  The Trick Is to Keep Breathing.
WILLIAM H. GASS, *Cartesian Sonata
  and Other Novellas.*
  Finding a Form.
  A Temple of Texts.
  The Tunnel.
  Willie Masters' Lonesome Wife.
GÉRARD GAVARRY, *Hoppla! 1 2 3.*
ETIENNE GILSON,
  The Arts of the Beautiful.
  Forms and Substances in the Arts.
C. S. GISCOMBE, *Giscome Road.*
  Here.
DOUGLAS GLOVER, *Bad News of the Heart.*
WITOLD GOMBROWICZ,
  A Kind of Testament.
PAULO EMÍLIO SALES GOMES, *P's Three
  Women.*
GEORGI GOSPODINOV, *Natural Novel.*
JUAN GOYTISOLO, *Count Julian.*
  Juan the Landless.
  Makbara.
  Marks of Identity.

FOR A FULL LIST OF PUBLICATIONS, VISIT:
www.dalkeyarchive.com

SELECTED DALKEY ARCHIVE TITLES

Henry Green, *Back.*
Blindness.
Concluding.
Doting.
Nothing.
Jack Green, *Fire the Bastards!*
Jiří Gruša, *The Questionnaire.*
Mela Hartwig, *Am I a Redundant Human Being?*
John Hawkes, *The Passion Artist.*
Whistlejacket.
Elizabeth Heighway, ed., *Contemporary Georgian Fiction.*
Aleksandar Hemon, ed., *Best European Fiction.*
Aidan Higgins, *Balcony of Europe.*
Blind Man's Bluff
Bornholm Night-Ferry.
Flotsam and Jetsam.
Langrishe, Go Down.
Scenes from a Receding Past.
Keizo Hino, *Isle of Dreams.*
Kazushi Hosaka, *Plainsong.*
Aldous Huxley, *Antic Hay.*
Crome Yellow.
Point Counter Point.
Those Barren Leaves.
Time Must Have a Stop.
Naoyuki Ii, *The Shadow of a Blue Cat.*
Gert Jonke, *The Distant Sound.*
Geometric Regional Novel.
Homage to Czerny.
The System of Vienna.
Jacques Jouet, *Mountain R.*
Savage.
Upstaged.
Mieko Kanai, *The Word Book.*
Yoram Kaniuk, *Life on Sandpaper.*
Hugh Kenner, *Flaubert.*
Joyce and Beckett: The Stoic Comedians.
Joyce's Voices.
Danilo Kiš, *The Attic.*
Garden, Ashes.
The Lute and the Scars
Psalm 44.
A Tomb for Boris Davidovich.
Anita Konkka, *A Fool's Paradise.*
George Konrád, *The City Builder.*
Tadeusz Konwicki, *A Minor Apocalypse.*
The Polish Complex.
Menis Koumandareas, *Koula.*
Elaine Kraf, *The Princess of 72nd Street.*
Jim Krusoe, *Iceland.*
Ayşe Kulin, *Farewell: A Mansion in Occupied Istanbul.*
Emilio Lascano Tegui, *On Elegance While Sleeping.*
Eric Laurrent, *Do Not Touch.*
Violette Leduc, *La Bâtarde.*
Edouard Levé, *Autoportrait.*
Suicide.
Mario Levi, *Istanbul Was a Fairy Tale.*
Deborah Levy, *Billy and Girl.*
José Lezama Lima, *Paradiso.*
Rosa Liksom, *Dark Paradise.*
Osman Lins, *Avalovara.*
The Queen of the Prisons of Greece.
Alf Mac Lochlainn, *The Corpus in the Library.*
Out of Focus.
Ron Loewinsohn, *Magnetic Field(s).*
Mina Loy, *Stories and Essays of Mina Loy.*
D. Keith Mano, *Take Five.*
Micheline Aharonian Marcom, *The Mirror in the Well.*
Ben Marcus, *The Age of Wire and String.*
Wallace Markfield, *Teitlebaum's Window.*
To an Early Grave.
David Markson, *Reader's Block.*
Wittgenstein's Mistress.
Carole Maso, *AVA.*
Ladislav Matejka and Krystyna Pomorska, eds., *Readings in Russian Poetics: Formalist and Structuralist Views.*
Harry Mathews, *Cigarettes.*
The Conversions.
The Human Country: New and Collected Stories.
The Journalist.
My Life in CIA.
Singular Pleasures.
The Sinking of the Odradek Stadium.
Tlooth.
Joseph McElroy, *Night Soul and Other Stories.*
Abdelwahab Meddeb, *Talismano.*
Gerhard Meier, *Isle of the Dead.*
Herman Melville, *The Confidence-Man.*
Amanda Michalopoulou, *I'd Like.*
Steven Millhauser, *The Barnum Museum.*
In the Penny Arcade.
Ralph J. Mills, Jr., *Essays on Poetry.*
Momus, *The Book of Jokes.*
Christine Montalbetti, *The Origin of Man.*
Western.
Olive Moore, *Spleen.*
Nicholas Mosley, *Accident.*
Assassins.
Catastrophe Practice.
Experience and Religion.
A Garden of Trees.
Hopeful Monsters.
Imago Bird.
Impossible Object.
Inventing God.
Judith.
Look at the Dark.
Natalie Natalia.
Serpent.
Time at War.
Warren Motte, *Fables of the Novel: French Fiction since 1990.*
Fiction Now: The French Novel in the 21st Century.
Oulipo: A Primer of Potential Literature.
Gerald Murnane, *Barley Patch.*
Inland.
Yves Navarre, *Our Share of Time.*
Sweet Tooth.
Dorothy Nelson, *In Night's City.*
Tar and Feathers.
Eshkol Nevo, *Homesick.*
Wilfrido D. Nolledo, *But for the Lovers.*
Flann O'Brien, *At Swim-Two-Birds.*
The Best of Myles.
The Dalkey Archive.
The Hard Life.
The Poor Mouth.

FOR A FULL LIST OF PUBLICATIONS, VISIT:
www.dalkeyarchive.com

SELECTED DALKEY ARCHIVE TITLES

The Third Policeman.
CLAUDE OLLIER, *The Mise-en-Scène.*
Wert and the Life Without End.
GIOVANNI ORELLI, *Walaschek's Dream.*
PATRIK OUŘEDNÍK, *Europeana.*
The Opportune Moment, 1855.
BORIS PAHOR, *Necropolis.*
FERNANDO DEL PASO, *News from the Empire.*
Palinuro of Mexico.
ROBERT PINGET, *The Inquisitory.*
Mahu or The Material.
Trio.
MANUEL PUIG, *Betrayed by Rita Hayworth.*
The Buenos Aires Affair.
Heartbreak Tango.
RAYMOND QUENEAU, *The Last Days.*
Odile.
Pierrot Mon Ami.
Saint Glinglin.
ANN QUIN, *Berg.*
Passages.
Three.
Tripticks.
ISHMAEL REED, *The Free-Lance Pallbearers.*
The Last Days of Louisiana Red.
Ishmael Reed: The Plays.
Juice!
Reckless Eyeballing.
The Terrible Threes.
The Terrible Twos.
Yellow Back Radio Broke-Down.
JASIA REICHARDT, *15 Journeys Warsaw to London.*
NOËLLE REVAZ, *With the Animals.*
JOÃO UBALDO RIBEIRO, *House of the Fortunate Buddhas.*
JEAN RICARDOU, *Place Names.*
RAINER MARIA RILKE, *The Notebooks of Malte Laurids Brigge.*
JULIÁN RÍOS, *The House of Ulysses.*
Larva: A Midsummer Night's Babel.
Poundemonium.
Procession of Shadows.
AUGUSTO ROA BASTOS, *I the Supreme.*
DANIËL ROBBERECHTS, *Arriving in Avignon.*
JEAN ROLIN, *The Explosion of the Radiator Hose.*
OLIVIER ROLIN, *Hotel Crystal.*
ALIX CLEO ROUBAUD, *Alix's Journal.*
JACQUES ROUBAUD, *The Form of a City Changes Faster, Alas, Than the Human Heart.*
The Great Fire of London.
Hortense in Exile.
Hortense Is Abducted.
The Loop.
Mathematics:
The Plurality of Worlds of Lewis.
The Princess Hoppy.
Some Thing Black.
RAYMOND ROUSSEL, *Impressions of Africa.*
VEDRANA RUDAN, *Night.*
STIG SÆTERBAKKEN, *Siamese.*
Self Control.
LYDIE SALVAYRE, *The Company of Ghosts.*
The Lecture.
The Power of Flies.
LUIS RAFAEL SÁNCHEZ, *Macho Camacho's Beat.*
SEVERO SARDUY, *Cobra & Maitreya.*

NATHALIE SARRAUTE, *Do You Hear Them?*
Martereau.
The Planetarium.
ARNO SCHMIDT, *Collected Novellas.*
Collected Stories.
Nobodaddy's Children.
Two Novels.
ASAF SCHURR, *Motti.*
GAIL SCOTT, *My Paris.*
DAMION SEARLS, *What We Were Doing and Where We Were Going.*
JUNE AKERS SEESE, *Is This What Other Women Feel Too?*
What Waiting Really Means.
BERNARD SHARE, *Inish.*
Transit.
VIKTOR SHKLOVSKY, *Bowstring.*
Knight's Move.
A Sentimental Journey: Memoirs 1917–1922.
Energy of Delusion: A Book on Plot.
Literature and Cinematography.
Theory of Prose.
Third Factory.
Zoo, or Letters Not about Love.
PIERRE SINIAC, *The Collaborators.*
KJERSTI A. SKOMSVOLD, *The Faster I Walk, the Smaller I Am.*
JOSEF ŠKVORECKÝ, *The Engineer of Human Souls.*
GILBERT SORRENTINO, *Aberration of Starlight.*
Blue Pastoral.
Crystal Vision.
Imaginative Qualities of Actual Things.
Mulligan Stew.
Pack of Lies.
Red the Fiend.
The Sky Changes.
Something Said.
Splendide-Hôtel.
Steelwork.
Under the Shadow.
W. M. SPACKMAN, *The Complete Fiction.*
ANDRZEJ STASIUK, *Dukla.*
Fado.
GERTRUDE STEIN, *The Making of Americans.*
A Novel of Thank You.
LARS SVENDSEN, *A Philosophy of Evil.*
PIOTR SZEWC, *Annihilation.*
GONÇALO M. TAVARES, *Jerusalem.*
Joseph Walser's Machine.
Learning to Pray in the Age of Technique.
LUCIAN DAN TEODOROVICI, *Our Circus Presents . . .*
NIKANOR TERATOLOGEN, *Assisted Living.*
STEFAN THEMERSON, *Hobson's Island.*
The Mystery of the Sardine.
Tom Harris.
TAEKO TOMIOKA, *Building Waves.*
JOHN TOOMEY, *Sleepwalker.*
JEAN-PHILIPPE TOUSSAINT, *The Bathroom.*
Camera.
Monsieur.
Reticence.
Running Away.
Self-Portrait Abroad.
Television.
The Truth about Marie.

FOR A FULL LIST OF PUBLICATIONS, VISIT:
www.dalkeyarchive.com

SELECTED DALKEY ARCHIVE TITLES

DUMITRU TSEPENEAG, *Hotel Europa.*
   The Necessary Marriage.
   Pigeon Post.
   Vain Art of the Fugue.
ESTHER TUSQUETS, *Stranded.*
DUBRAVKA UGRESIC, *Lend Me Your Character.*
   Thank You for Not Reading.
TOR ULVEN, *Replacement.*
MATI UNT, *Brecht at Night.*
   Diary of a Blood Donor.
   Things in the Night.
ÁLVARO URIBE AND OLIVIA SEARS, EDS.,
   Best of Contemporary Mexican Fiction.
ELOY URROZ, *Friction.*
   The Obstacles.
LUISA VALENZUELA, *Dark Desires and the Others.*
   He Who Searches.
PAUL VERHAEGHEN, *Omega Minor.*
AGLAJA VETERANYI, *Why the Child Is Cooking in the Polenta.*
BORIS VIAN, *Heartsnatcher.*
LLORENÇ VILLALONGA, *The Dolls' Room.*
TOOMAS VINT, *An Unending Landscape.*
ORNELA VORPSI, *The Country Where No One Ever Dies.*
AUSTRYN WAINHOUSE, *Hedyphagetica.*
CURTIS WHITE, *America's Magic Mountain.*
   The Idea of Home.
   Memories of My Father Watching TV.
   Requiem.

DIANE WILLIAMS, *Excitability: Selected Stories.*
   Romancer Erector.
DOUGLAS WOOLF, *Wall to Wall.*
   Ya! & John-Juan.
JAY WRIGHT, *Polynomials and Pollen.*
   The Presentable Art of Reading Absence.
PHILIP WYLIE, *Generation of Vipers.*
MARGUERITE YOUNG, *Angel in the Forest.*
   Miss MacIntosh, My Darling.
REYOUNG, *Unbabbling.*
VLADO ŽABOT, *The Succubus.*
ZORAN ŽIVKOVIĆ, *Hidden Camera.*
LOUIS ZUKOFSKY, *Collected Fiction.*
VITOMIL ZUPAN, *Minuet for Guitar.*
SCOTT ZWIREN, *God Head.*

FOR A FULL LIST OF PUBLICATIONS, VISIT:
www.dalkeyarchive.com